G R JORDAN

Macleod's Cruise

The great difference between voyages
rests not with the ships, but with the
people you meet on them.

AMELIA A. BARR

Contents

Foreword

The events of this book, while based around real locations around Inverness, are entirely fictional and all characters do not represent any living or deceased person. All companies are fictitious representations. It's a bit of blether!

Acknowledgement

To Ken, Jean, Colin, Evelyn, John and Rosemary for your work in bringing this novel to completion, your time and effort is deeply appreciated.

Books by G R Jordan

The Highlands and Islands Detective series (Crime)

1. Water's Edge
2. The Bothy
3. The Horror Weekend
4. The Small Ferry
5. Dead at Third Man
6. The Pirate Club
7. A Personal Agenda
8. A Just Punishment
9. The Numerous Deaths of Santa Claus
10. Our Gated Community
11. The Satchel
12. Culhwch Alpha
13. Fair Market Value
14. The Coach Bomber
15. The Culling at Singing Sands
16. Where Justice Fails
17. The Cortado Club
18. Cleared to Die
19. Man Overboard!
20. Antisocial Behaviour
21. Rogues' Gallery
22. The Death of Macleod - Inferno Book 1

Kirsten Stewart Thrillers (Thriller)

Jac Moonshine Thrillers

1. Jac's Revenge
2. Jac for the People
3. Jac the Pariah

Siobhan Duffy Mysteries

1. A Giant Killing
2. Death of the Witch
3. The Bloodied Hands

The Contessa Munroe Mysteries (Cozy Mystery)

1. Corpse Reviver
2. Frostbite
3. Cobra's Fang

The Patrick Smythe Series (Crime)

1. The Disappearance of Russell Hadleigh
2. The Graves of Calgary Bay
3. The Fairy Pools Gathering

Austerley & Kirkgordon Series (Fantasy)

1. Crescendo!
2. The Darkness at Dillingham
3. Dagon's Revenge
4. Ship of Doom

Supernatural and Elder Threat Assessment Agency (SETAA) Series (Fantasy)

1. Scarlett O'Meara: Beastmaster

Island Adventures Series (Cosy Fantasy Adventure)

1. Surface Tensions

Dark Wen Series (Horror Fantasy)

1. The Blasphemous Welcome
2. The Demon's Chalice

Chapter 01

Agnes was getting too old for this. She spent most of her life on cruise ships, toing and froing between her life back on shore and the daily work grudge when she was on board. It might've been different if her dreams had come true of being an entertainer. Playing every night in the ship's theatre, or even running one of the kids' activity clubs, would have been great. Even taking the passengers ashore, showing them the various parts of the world that, although she toured, she never really got to see properly.

Instead, Agnes spent the time that they were ashore cleaning up bedrooms, tidying bunks. At least she was doing the posh rooms. They were classy. Not just a couple of drop-down beds, an elongated box. These state rooms had something about them. Separate sleeping quarters and a large balcony outside. Although some guests could be strange, leaving the cabins in a rather peculiar state, the majority were businesspeople or other well-thought-of citizens.

They had a type of glamour to them, and Agnes enjoyed seeing it. They tipped well too, which was always a bonus, and occasionally she got to see someone who was almost famous. It was that actress. The girl could've only have been what—

twenty-one? Long blonde hair. She'd been running around in a skimpy outfit, her boyfriend with her.

Agnes remembered when she had a body like that. Well, no, she didn't, but she had a better body than she did now. Back when she was young and happy with herself. She had cleaned too many bathrooms, hoovered too many floors now to have a body that was good for anything. It just felt sore.

But she was here to make some beds, and she needed to see if the cabin was clear. She pressed the buzzer on the outside and stood patiently, waiting. There came no answer, so she rang again. Once more, no answer, so she rapped the door with her hand. On the third time of receiving no answer, she took her key card and accessed the room.

Opening the door, she shouted through, 'Housekeeping,' and then shuffled inside, bringing her small trolley of cleaning goods with her. She looked around the room and gave a smile. There was the large balcony at the far end, the door to which was open. At least she wouldn't have to air the cabin. She walked over towards it, looking out at the empty sea beyond.

If they were a day out of port, there'd be another few days before they'd reach the next one. Far out to sea and away, the occupants of the cabin wouldn't be off on a visit to anywhere. They'd be enjoying the pool, the casino, the library, the coffee shops, the food, all the myriad of distractions that there were on board. If Agnes was quick, she could get this done before they even thought about returning.

She stepped over towards the balcony door, aware that it was fully open and the wind coming through was quite strong. There was usually a breeze, because the vessel was on the move, but then she looked down at the floor. It was slightly wet.

Agnes bent down and touched it. There had been no rain,

had there? *Bizarre*, she thought. It wasn't so wet that you'd thought somebody had thrown a bucket of water down. More sort of accidental spillage or damp feet. Enough though that it hadn't evaporated yet.

Agnes ignored this, took out a cloth and some polish, and wiped down the table and the furniture around the stateroom. The bedrooms were up a little staircase where she would find a large double bed. It was in a spacious cabin, along with a walk-in cloakroom where you could store clothing. There was also a small study up there.

Yes, if Agnes was going to cruise, she would do it in this type of cabin. Away from the riffraff. Away from those who would have their pesky kids shouting. Agnes wouldn't go cruising with children. She would go with a man who would pay her attention, or at least a man with plenty of money. If he wasn't interesting, she could always pop down to the casino.

She'd watched, occasionally, the real high rollers in the casino. There were the tourists who popped along, with maybe fifty quid, and there were tables for them to enjoy themselves. Yet, now and then, you got some real high roller who would blow five grand in a night. That was the sort of man she wanted. A man who could keep her accustomed to the ways that she'd like to get accustomed to and never had.

Agnes chortled as she continued her duties. There were a couple of glasses, and they seemed to have been used last night. A quick smell told her whisky had been in one, possibly gin in the other, but she took them and replaced them with others. Checking that all the drink canteens were full, she popped outside onto the balcony, giving it a wipe down. For a moment, she stood looking out to sea.

There were no other vessels around. Nothing except this

3

playground, vast as it was, cruising along through the sea. She peered down the side of the vessel. Below there were smaller balconies, tucked on the end of cabins. Other people wouldn't have a balcony at all. They'd be inside a place with two beds and a couple of fold-down bunks if you had kids as well. It meant you could cruise on a budget.

But not those in this stateroom. This person had money. She wondered who they were. Agnes never got told about them, never saw what their lifestyle was like. If she was lucky, she had the odd, very brief conversation. They asked Agnes what she did. She told them they were looking at it. They asked about her home. Well, Derek was home.

Derek had been a footballer. He'd been strong, rugged, and Agnes had fancied the backside off him. They got married, and tried to have kids in vain. Derek had changed from being a man with toned thighs, a strapping chest, and a caring heart, to a fat slob who sat watching television. He swore at referees and complained about how he should have made it if it wasn't for that shite on the telly.

What he hadn't done was go out and work properly for any part of his life. Agnes had hated it, and being a devout Catholic, had been told that she couldn't divorce him. She believed that, and so got a job on a cruise ship, spending half her life away from Derek. Despite it being the working part of her life, Agnes thought that this was the better half. At least she got to see a bit of glamour. She got to see the shows as well. Occasionally, in the winter months when they were out of season and things weren't so busy, she could get the odd ticket. A little perk this company ran. She'd worked for a few of them, but this vessel was the best. It was certainly the biggest she'd been on, and the food, even for the employees, was good.

Cruise ships all sailed under a flag, and depending on which flag they sailed under, the conditions for the employees could vary. The UK flag at least guaranteed decent food, workers' rights, sensible hours of work. Yes, she had to do her bit. They expected their pound of flesh, but they looked after you. Several times she'd been ill at sea, caught colds and been told to stay in bed. The doctor on board had seen to her. It was a half-decent life.

Agnes looked back out to sea, gave a smile, and turned back to her chores. She ran a quick hoover over downstairs. When she'd finished, she started doing the handrail that led up the stairs to the bedroom. There was only the one bedroom and a small study on the side. Agnes always laughed at that. Who needed a small study? Yet these business people would have their laptops set up there. If you owned your own company, you were never away, never free from it.

Agnes didn't like that idea, but that was okay. If her imagined husband owned it, he could look after the business. She could sun herself upstairs by the pool. Or she could be down in the casino. Or she could attend a show, eating a glamorous buffet, mingling with people from around the world who also had money. Agnes had dreams, but they were only dreams. In truth, she was happy, as long as she was away from Derek. *This life on the sea wasn't a bad one*, she thought.

It sounded like there was a noise, and Agnes froze suddenly. She looked around the stateroom but could see nothing. The door had been open, so she closed it, thinking the noise might've come from outside. But where from outside? Another passenger? Those noises often got lost when the ship was cruising along, and they weren't near to any land to hear anything else particularly loud.

Agnes stroked her chin, but then caught herself on. *What am I? Some sort of sleuth?* she thought. Instead, she grabbed the polish and the cloth, and went back to the stairs, making sure the handrails were coming up nicely. As she got towards the top of the stairs, she could hear the noise again.

'Hello? Anyone in? It's just the cleaning crew, just housekeeping. Sorry, I knocked. I've been here for a bit, I didn't realise. Hope I didn't catch you asleep. I'm sorry, if that's the case. Hello—anyone there?'

There was no sound at first, and then Agnes thought she heard a—well, she wasn't sure what it was. It was two things hitting. Almost a light dull thud. What on earth was that?

Agnes remembered back to a time when she was younger. She'd been cleaning, and she'd heard noises in the bedroom. She'd gone along and tapped, and there was silence. After doing it again, she'd convinced herself she'd heard something, so she pulled back the door to find out. She saw two people, frozen in the act of lovemaking.

The son of the occupants had brought his girlfriend in while mother and father were off at the pool, or casino, or somewhere on the boat. The young lady and he had decided to have some private time. Unfortunately, it wasn't private time the parents thought they should be having.

Agnes had stridden in, and when they'd seen her, they'd simply frozen. Agnes had been embarrassed, especially when the young man had thrown the woman off to one side, and come chasing up towards her. She remembered turning her back and asking him to put something on. She laughed. He had begged her not to tell his parents, and Agnes hadn't. She'd apologised, and said she'd leave, and then, when she'd got down to housekeeping, had burst out laughing. She'd found it romantic in some ways. It reminded her of better times with Derek. Early days.

But this didn't sound the same. This was disturbing. There it was again. That sort of dull click, that thud, that—what was it? Agnes banged on the bedroom door.

'This is housekeeping. Is everything okay in there? Is there anyone in? Please answer. I don't want to barge in on you, but I need to make sure things are okay.'

There was no reply, except for that dull thud. Agnes stopped and listened. She looked at her wristwatch. Yes, there was the thud. She waited. There was the thud again. Then one more time. The interval between them being—well, it must be about the same. What on earth?

They'd taught Agnes that if she thought something was wrong, she should check it out. Always better to assume the worst, realise it isn't, and then apologise. She had learnt to deal with passengers over time, and most appreciated your efforts to keep them safe. The odd one or two didn't, but it didn't matter. This was important. She needed to make sure something wasn't wrong in that bedroom.

Agnes banged on the door once more. 'This is housekeeping. I'm coming in. If you're not in a decent state, please grab a sheet.'

She nearly burst out laughing at the memory of the young man and his lady coming to mind. Agnes pushed open the door and froze. The bedroom had a double bed off to the left as she entered. In the middle of the room was a fan, and although the ceiling wasn't overly high, it was much higher than the other cabins.

Normally, Agnes would have walked in, took a step to the left, and cleaned the floor around there before looking to the ensuite and the walk-in wardrobe on the right. However, dominating the room was a man.

He was attached to the fan by what looked like a fancy tie. It was snaked around his neck and then around the fan, which was turning. It spun him gently round, but clearly was struggling with his weight.

Whether or not the fan had couped to one side, it was stuttering. Agnes realised that the thud she was hearing were the man's feet coming together at that stutter before being moved apart again as he continued to swing.

She raised a hand to her mouth and stared. The man's face was unmoving, his eyes closed. He could have been around her age. She hadn't cleaned this cabin on this voyage, and she didn't know who he was, but she could tell from the cabin that he hadn't been alone. He had a partner with him wherever she was.

Agnes wondered, should she bring him down? Should she try to cut him down? Was he dead? Surely, he was dead.

She stepped forward, ducking under the feet, and not knowing what else to do, she swung her left hand up, catching the man around the backside.

'Mister, are you alive? Please tell me you're alive! Are you? Tell me!'

She stepped backwards, away from the swinging feet as he rotated. There was absolutely no sign of life from the man. She turned and ran down the stairs. Her heart was pounding, but her head was telling her to focus.

Dead body in the cabin. What should I do?

She took her cleaning cart, pulled it to the entrance to the stateroom, opened the door and pulled the cart outside. She put the cart across the door after it closed and erected her signs that said closed for cleaning.

Slowly, Agnes walked down the corridor and found a phone. Calling housekeeping, she reported the situation quietly, leaving out the detail of the swinging feet, but simply saying there was a dead body. Having done so, Agnes walked back to the cabin and stood in front of the cart that blocked the entrance.

She would wait. Her hands ran through each other as she stood, praying that someone would come quickly. As Agnes tried to focus on something else, someone walked past, and she smiled and said hello. Inside, she felt her heart thump. She felt everything else shake.

He was dead. She couldn't get rid of the look. She couldn't get rid of what she'd seen. Even with his eyes closed, the man's face had been a picture of horror.

Chapter 02

'Seoras, would you sit your backside down?'

Macleod turned and threw a stare at his partner, Jane. A bead of sweat ran down his forehead and he looked up at the glass dome covering the swimming pool. Outside, the air temperature wasn't high, but the sun beaming down through the glass meant that the swimming pool area was almost tropical.

Macleod wasn't a keen fan of weather that was too hot. He'd grown up in Scotland after all. Born and bred on the isle of Lewis, which being surrounded by water, was moderated paradise. The sea kept the temperature somewhere between zero and fifteen degrees for most of the year. When temperatures rose to the upper teens, people there would wear simple shirts or even strip down on the beach to go for a swim. The idea of constant temperatures in the thirties scared any man from the Hebrides. His partner, Jane, however, seemed to lap up the heat.

'Get your book. Sit down with your book and read. You're relaxing, remember? This is us away. This is a chill-out cruise,' said Jane. 'This is why we came here. You can't run off and investigate something. Can't drag me around former criminal hot spots. You can't disappear off and have a word with a suspect that got away. Yes, I remember that one. Take me on holiday and then do that. Oh, why does he suddenly want to go here? I remember that, Seoras Macleod. You still haven't paid me back for that one.'

Macleod raised his eyebrows. But she was right. He had done that because he had to let the woman know. She'd murdered people. She would face judgement one day, not in this life, but in another, and he needed to warn her of that. He needed to tell her he knew—he just couldn't prove it in the court of law.

Macleod looked down at the black trunks he was wearing. They went down to his knees. On top, he wore a shirt that was sitting open. He buttoned it up. It was a summer shirt. Jane had undone the buttons, telling him he would not be out and about as he was going to sit by a pool. She then told him he should swim, told him he should sit in the sauna, told him he could try the jacuzzi, then told him to read his bloody book. At that point, he'd sat down because she'd sworn.

Jane was, well, while she was a feisty woman, she was very tolerant, but when she got really worked up, the odd word would come out. Never coarse, just a 'bloody' or a 'blooming'. None of those other words, but that was her annoyed. He didn't want to annoy her because, in truth, she deserved this trip.

It had been a rough time. His mental capacities had got shaken. He had seen a man in his head, a man who was thankfully now gone. Jane had suggested they go away because they needed the break. Times had been tough, and Macleod had no intentions of going away.

He was now going to be running two separate teams. Clarissa had moved over to the art world, and he was just 'keeping an eye on her' while she was up in Inverness. Hope was his detective inspector running the murder team. Macleod had become more of a supervisory figure. It had been inevitable, although he would rather always be in the thick of an investigation. He had to fight sometimes to let Hope take over.

She was capable, more than capable, and he was glad for the team. Ross was about to take his sergeant's exams. He'd have DI McGrath, DS Ross, and DC Cunningham. Patterson had moved over to be with Clarissa. She was now being moved up to DI as well. *God help the art world*, he thought. Macleod didn't say that as a blasphemy. He genuinely prayed it.

Macleod sat down, not on a lounger, but on a chair with a table in front of him. He pulled out the reading device. Jane had insisted he didn't bring books. Macleod wasn't a great reader of books, but those he had were bulky. She had gone through them. Several were cases. Unsolved crimes. He said he was just trying to keep his mind fresh, but she had deposited them back on the shelf and turned up the next day with a reading device. He had looked at it. It was thin, glass on one side, and he flipped it open.

'Twenty thousand books you can get in there,' Jane had said.

'Where are we cruising to?' he had retorted. He thought she would laugh at that, but he could see that this idea of hers was one he would have to take seriously. That evening they sat down, and on a computer, they'd picked out over fifty pounds' worth of books to stick onto this device. Macleod was still bemused by it. Twenty thousand books. Who could read twenty thousand books?

He had tried it that night in bed and found that he'd switched it off after three minutes. He hadn't used it much before coming away, but now he was here, and at those times when he was told to sit down and rest, Jane told him to read.

In a way, she was right. He couldn't just sit and rest. That wasn't Macleod, and at other times, he would leave her sunning herself or perusing the shops in the ship's main arcade, while he went off for a walk around. He'd actually spent some time in the casino, though he had spent no money.

Casinos were not moral places to Macleod. People were blowing money that they could simply spend on something useful or give away to the poor. Seoras had been in enough casinos and gambling dens in his time to have been quite taken by the strategies used. He would never ever spend any of his own money, or indeed anyone else's, but he would stand and watch. He felt he could make money if he tried, but he knew that was the trap. The house always wins in the long run.

They'd also been to shows on board, seen magic tricks and various other pieces of entertainment. Their cabin was on the outside of the vessel and had a small balcony. There was one room with a bed, a table, and it wasn't exactly cramped, but Macleod thought that he'd like more room. It was the only place of true privacy. He'd spent some time in the library until Jane caught him looking at some real crime books. After that, any visits to the library had been supervised, and he had to take the device with him to read.

It had been good, though. Jane was feeling relaxed, and in truth, he had wound down. He needed this break, his body needed this break, and they needed the break.

The vessel was due to spend another three days at sea before setting into a port. He liked those days where he got to walk around and see something, even though most of it, he wasn't that bothered with. He was no history buff, but they strolled along, had lunch out, took in the sights and spent time together, somewhere away from Inverness. Time was a precious commodity, Macleod realised, the older he got. With the mental distress he'd suffered previously, he wondered just how much longer he would be in his full faculties. How much longer he would have his health? How much longer would Jane? One never knew and so at times like these, you had to take everything on board.

Macleod scanned over the top of his device, watching those around the swimming pool. He heard a cough. 'Read the damn thing, Seoras.'

'I am,' he said.

'No, you're not. Read it. Don't lie to me! Just read it.'

Macleod's eyes shot down to the screen. He didn't know where on the screen he'd left last time, but he left his eyes there until he felt Jane's were no longer looking at him. He cast a glance back up and scanned the other side of the pool. There was a woman there being approached by one of the cruise staff.

The member of staff in question was a woman of maybe thirty, sporting long blonde hair, and dressed in a rather smart shirt. She had epaulets with gold. Macleod saw the woman being approached suddenly went white in the face, the colour draining fast. Were there tears? The woman was escorted away quickly, a towel wrapped around her, and she disappeared from the poolside area.

'Entertainment's over. Would you read the book?' said Jane.

Macleod nodded, knowing better than to argue. He started to read and wondered how he'd got to the French Revolution. It wasn't a history book. It was a tale set in the past, but he couldn't remember how it started. How many people did this, read, taking nothing in?

He was sure the story was probably good. The writer certainly came well recommended, but Seoras didn't have a clue what was going on. He was tuning out. Every now and again, he would look left or right. He'd find someone of interest. That was the thing. He read people; he didn't read books. Books never helped him solve cases.

No, that was wrong. Books could help you solve things. You had to go into books and look at times. That's if he didn't have a Ross. Ross was good at finding stuff out. Nowadays, all that stuff was on the computer, wasn't it?

In truth, he was missing it. The thrill of the chase, the hunt, the brainstorming, the working it out. He lived for it and yet he knew he should be shot of it. He knew there should come a point at which he should leave it all behind, lest he become wholly consumed. At some point, it would be too much.

He wanted Jane to have somebody there, somebody she could rely on and could enjoy her later years with. She had said to him it was maybe time to give it up. He'd been thinking about it for several years, but never did he want to go through with it.

'If you will not read it, at least get me a drink.'

The device was put down instantly, and Macleod stood up, smiling. 'What do you want?'

'Surprise me.'

'What, like with a tea?'

Jane looked up at him. 'We're on a cruise ship. You're going to surprise me with a tea. With what? You going to get me an Earl Grey. I said, "Surprise me," Seoras.'

'Alcoholic?' he asked.

'Yes,' said Jane. 'Something alcoholic. Surprise me.'

Macleod walked over to the bar at the far end of the swimming pool. He stood in line for a moment and then, when it came to his turn, he looked up at the drinks' menu behind the waiter.

'I'll have a latte,' he said. 'My partner wants me to surprise her, something alcoholic.'

'What sort of thing does she like?'

'I don't know. We don't drink much.'

'Right,' said the man. 'What sort of flavours would she go for?'

'We drink coffee.'

'Right,' he said. 'I really could do with a wee bit more help.'

Macleod looked at the names of the drinks on the menu. Tom Collins, that was classy, wasn't it? Maybe a Tom Collins would be a good one. Pina Colada, that was another good one. Sex on the beach. He shook his head, moving down to the next one, and then he stopped. *She said, 'Surprise me,'* he thought, *This will surprise her.*

'I'll have sex on the beach,' said Macleod, almost proud of himself for announcing this.

Then he suddenly panicked. 'What's in that?' he asked.

'Shot of peach schnapps, orange juice, cranberry juice,' said the waiter.

Macleod watched him make it, looking at the red bottom changing colour slowly up into the yellow top. There was a slice of orange on the top, a straw sticking out of it. Although he was never a man for alcohol, he could see the attraction of the colours.

A mug was put down beside him. It was a classy mug, in fairness, containing the brown liquid. He turned to walk back to Jane. The mug in one hand, the glass in the other, but saw a woman talking to Jane. It was the blonde woman with the epaulettes in the white shirt. She turned and walked towards him.

'Would you be Detective Inspector Macleod?' she asked.

'Detective Chief Inspector Macleod,' he said, 'but it's fine. I'm actually on holiday.'

'Yes, sir,' said the woman. 'Most people on the cruise ship are on holiday unless they're working as part of the team.'

'Of course,' said Macleod. 'Can I help?'

'The Master, sir, that would be the Captain, he's asking if you could come and assist him.'

'I don't really know anything about boats.'

'The vessel, sir, is not what he wants help with. I'm afraid there's been a death and the Master would like your help.'

'Is this an official request?'

'We've perused the people on board and we have a constable from another country. You're the only officer of the law that we have on board from the UK and the Master was quite impressed that it was you. He's asked for your assistance if you'd be so kind.'

'Just a moment,' said Macleod. He walked past the woman and over to Jane, sitting at the table. 'Sex on the beach,' he said.

She almost laughed, but then she looked over at the blonde woman standing a little distance away.

'What does she want? She was looking for the Detective Inspector.' Jane's face grimaced.

'She said they have a death on board and the Master of the vessel wants me to have a look.'

'Is it suspicious?'

'I don't know,' said Macleod. 'They haven't told me yet, but if they're asking for a police officer, I'd suspect there'd be something about it.'

'Why can't we just have one holiday? Why can't we just go away somewhere? I mean, we're in the middle of the sea,' said Jane.

'If you want, I'll say no.'

She stood up, took the drink off him, setting it down on the table and took his latte too.

'You won't have time for that, and I'm going to need that one,' she said. She put her arms around him and kissed him on the side of the cheek. 'I'm married to a policeman and there is no way Seoras Macleod is going to turn down a request about a suspicious death. If you do, you will sit here and you will wonder what's going on and you will try to find out by other methods. Look to it, help them, and try to do it as quick as you can. I'll be here.'

'Thank you,' said Macleod. He kissed her back on the lips, then turned and walked over to the blonde-haired member of the crew.

'Seoras!'

He turned back and saw a devious look on Jane's face. 'Sex on the beach. That's a promise as soon as we make land.' It was said out loud. Very loudly. Macleod could see others looking at him, a few sniggers and a few shocked faces. Jane was nearly beginning to cry with laughter.

'You better find a beach and a secluded one,' he said, before turning round to the blonde-haired woman.

'Well,' he said, 'Something to look forward to. I'm all yours. Take me to your Master.'

Chapter 03

'Detective Chief Inspector,' said the blonde woman as they walked, 'I'm the ship's Third Officer, Melanie Thatcher, and I'll take you to meet Captain Fraser. He's the Master of the vessel. Unfortunately, one of our passengers has died, and the circumstances seem reasonably suspicious. As I said, I believe the Captain would like someone with more knowledge of these affairs to take a look.'

'When you say, "Take a look,"' asked Macleod, 'am I investigating officially?'

'You're on a British vessel, Detective Chief Inspector.'

'Please, just call me Seoras or Macleod, or Inspector, if you must. Probably best just to call me Seoras at the moment. We don't want to get any of the passengers worried.'

'That's a good idea, Seoras,' said the young woman. 'Call me Melanie. Mel, if you wish.'

'What was the name of the deceased person?'

'I believe the Captain's going to take you through all of that. He's up on the bridge at the moment. We'll go there, and he'll escort. I'm going to take over the watch of the vessel.'

'Very good,' said Macleod. 'Does this happen often?'

'It's a first for me, but I'm not as long in the tooth at sea as the Captain. He's had plenty years on the waves. I'm not sure if he's seen a suspicious death before. He's certainly seen several people pass while on the cruises. The age range of our passengers is on the older end of the scale. It's always a possibility, or some sort of medical emergency.'

Macleod was led to a lift and then up to the bridge of the ship. As he entered and looked aghast at the many dials and displays that there were, a man turned and hastened towards him. He was dressed in smart black trousers and a white shirt with epaulettes, but with a lot of gold on them.

'Detective Chief Inspector Macleod, can I just say, thank you for agreeing to come. My name's Captain Fraser. I'm the Master of the ship, and I'll take you to have a look at the scene we're faced with. Thank you, Melanie,' he said to the young woman beyond Macleod.

'I've never actually investigated on a ship,' said Macleod, 'and I was just saying to Melanie, probably best if you call me Seoras. We don't want the passengers to get excited that there's a police officer investigating.'

'Indeed. Maybe you'd call me Alan then.'

'No, Captain. You're the Captain of the ship and I'll call you Captain. I don't think the passengers will find that strange.'

'As you will. Seoras, where does that come from?' he asked, suddenly.

'Scotland, from the Isle of Lewis. Some people say it's Gaelic for George, but I've never seen it that way. Just Seoras.'

'Well, let me say, I'm sorry to break up your holiday. Hopefully, there isn't anything too suspicious about this. I'll take you down to the cabin now. The deceased man is a Mr Kilmartin. I know little else beyond that for now. His wife, Mrs Kilmartin, has been informed. She's not in her room. We've taken her elsewhere, and the ship's counsellor is with her. The ship's doctor I've asked to meet with us at the cabin.

'I appreciate that when you investigate murders, you have a team with you and no doubt, specialists. We don't have anyone of that ilk. I checked the passenger manifest to see if we had any other officers, but we have no one of your level, indeed no other English-speaking police officers. The other police on board are from different nationalities, and I thought it wiser to ask you if you wanted them rather than bring you all together.'

'I think at the moment we'll stick with it as being me until we've got an initial assessment. These days, I'm sure with ship communications, I can speak to my colleagues back in Scotland.'

'Oh, undoubtedly,' said the Captain. 'We'll give you every help in that, obviously, if it's required, but let's get to the cabin first—see what you think.'

Macleod followed the Captain to the lift and then round various corridors after the short descent. He realised he was quite high on the ship.

'It's happened in a more sort of exclusive area of the vessel,' said the Captain. 'These cabins, they're not cheap. They're at the top end, and that's quite alarming to me. There's the potential that it may have been suicide.'

Macleod followed the Captain along the corridor until they came to a door. It was guarded by a man in another white shirt and black trousers combination, but with slightly less gold on his epaulettes.

'Jones,' said the Captain. 'Thank you. Anyone been around?'

'The doctor's inside. Agnes is inside as well, the housekeeper.'

'The housekeeper?' asked Macleod.

'Yes,' said the Captain. 'Agnes found the body. I thought you'd want to speak to her. The doctor's inside because we had to check if the man was dead and certify it. Beyond that, I've tried not to let anyone in.'

'Good,' said Macleod. The Captain opened the door and the pair of them entered the cabin. Sitting down on a long sofa was a woman in a cleaner's outfit, and sitting beside her was a man in a white shirt and black trousers.

'Inspector, this is Agnes Corden, one of our housekeepers and who found Mr Kilmartin. This is Dr Felix.'

'Thank you both,' said Macleod. 'I'm sorry to talk to you in these circumstances, but we have what we have. If I could speak briefly to Agnes first and then, doctor, if you'll accompany me to the body, we'll talk there.'

'Of course,' said the Captain and stood behind Macleod. Macleod looked at Agnes, who was now trembling slightly.

'Doctor, has Agnes had anything to drink? A cup of tea or anything?'

'We've just been waiting. She said she was okay,' said the doctor, but was now gazing at her.

'Maybe a cup of tea or something,' said Macleod. 'She seems to be in a bit of shock. That's perfectly normal, Agnes,' said Macleod. 'Even people in my line of work, it happens to. The Captain says you're the housekeeper. Are you part of a team?'

'Yes. Yes, Inspector.'

'Seoras,' said Macleod, eager to try to put the woman at her ease. Macleod was aware that he was still dressed in trunks and a shirt, which he had done up, but he looked like a holidaymaker and not an inspector.

'I'm part of the housekeeping team,' said Agnes. 'It's the first time I've done this cabin, but I do a lot of the cabins, the more

22

expensive ones. I don't know what to say.'

'Just take me through arriving, what you did, what you saw,' said Macleod.

'Well, the thing is that I came in. Well, I knocked first. Rang the bell,' she said. 'Sorry, I'm getting a bit confused.'

'It's fine,' said Macleod. 'Take your time.'

'Well, I rang the bell twice, nobody answered. I then rapped the door with my hand. Nobody answered, so I opened the door with my keycard.'

'Sorry, Agnes. Captain, do these have locks the same as my cabin?'

'Yes, it's a passkey, so we can tell who's been in.'

'Okay, and who has been in?'

'Well, I need to check the system. Agnes, like all the housekeepers, has access, but they only have access to certain areas, which would be on their cleaning rota. They don't have access to everyone's room.'

'Anybody else who can get in?'

'Some of the senior staff have access, but we can check if they've used that access. Although, I'd be amazed if any of my staff were involved.'

'Just going through formalities,' said Macleod, and turned back to Agnes. 'So, you've rung, knocked, and you now come in.'

'Yes,' said Agnes. 'I came in and I shout "Housekeeping," and nobody answered, so I assume I'm on my own and get on with cleaning. I do a bit of dusting, do hoovering, but I didn't notice anything amiss when I came in. Oh, sorry, I should have said this first, shouldn't I? When I came in, the door was open to the balcony.'

'Okay,' said Macleod, 'is that normal?'

23

'Well, sometimes people leave it open, but this was fully open, and I thought to myself, I won't need to air the cabin.'

'And what did you do then?'

'Well, I went over and there was a slightly wet patch down there as well, and then I cleaned, Inspector. Oh, sorry, Seoras? Is that what you said?'

'Yes, it's Seoras, but Inspector's fine. Whatever is easiest for you,' said Macleod. 'Where did you clean?'

'Well, I hoovered, I dusted down here. I then started on the stairs. I did the banister, the railings, and that was when—well, I've been in at this point ten, maybe fifteen minutes, and then I heard a sound.'

'A sound?'

'Yes. It was like a thud, a dull thud, a quiet thud, every now and again, and it was rhythmical, so I thought, what should I do? Because it was coming from up near the bedroom. I . . .'

'So, what did you do?' asked Macleod.

'Well, I went up and rapped on the door,' said Agnes.

'And did you get any answer?'

'No, and then I opened the door and there he was. He was attached to the fan,' she said, 'by a tie.' Her eyes watered. 'And then, oh God, his feet, when he swung round, his feet would hit. That's what I'd heard, his feet hitting, and then . . .'

'It's okay, Agnes, take your time,' said Macleod.

'Well, I held myself together, and I went downstairs. I phoned it through, and I said, there's a dead body, and I put my cleaning cart in front of the door and I—well, I stood there until they came. And then, the doctor came in and I've sat downstairs since. Oh, God,' she blurted, and burst into tears. Macleod took her hand.

'It's okay, Agnes. You've had a shock. Captain,' he said, 'I'll need the doctor. Is there anyone else you can take Agnes to? Is there a team, a medical team?'

'Oh, yes, we have more than one doctor. I'll get someone to take her down.' The Captain then knelt beside Agnes.

'It's fine, Agnes,' he said. 'Don't worry, okay? Don't panic. You've done well. You've done really well. We're going to give you some time off now, and we'll see how you get on, but the staff, the medical staff, will look after you. I'll drop in later. Make sure you're okay.'

'Thank you, Captain,' she said, 'Thank you.' The Captain disappeared out into the corridor and a member of the crew was summoned. He took Agnes away. The doctor then led Macleod up the small flight of stairs that led to the bedroom. Macleod stood at the open door to the bedroom, a little bemused.

'He appears to be lying on the bed.'

'Yes, he is, Seoras,' said the doctor. 'The thing is that we had to see if he was still alive, so we took him down. Once we'd taken him down, we put him there. The tie on the bed, that's what he was hanging by, around the neck. You can see the abrasions on the neck.'

'Do we know for definite he was asphyxiated, that he died up there?'

'He definitely died of asphyxiation. I'm sorry, I'm not sure I could confirm it was definitely the tie.'

'How do you mean?' asked Macleod. 'If it wasn't the tie, what would it be?'

'I found that the markings around the neck, they're not fitting the tie exactly. We're not in a mortuary here, and I'm not a forensics expert. Yes, it looks like he died from asphyxiation. Whether that tie did it, I don't know. It might be best if I talk to your forensics people. I can do what I can to assist, but I need somebody to lead me, and I don't want to do anything to the body that would be detrimental to an investigation.'

'Okay,' said Macleod, 'I appreciate that.'

He walked into the room and looked around. Taking out a tissue from his shirt pocket, Macleod opened and closed drawers. He lifted the occasional object before putting it back down exactly where it was.

'Do you have anybody with a camera?' asked Macleod.

'We have cameras on board,' said the Captain. 'Why?'

'I'd like someone to come around and photograph here before we move anything.'

Macleod stepped forward into the alcove that served as a walk-in wardrobe. For a moment, he looked through everything, using his tissue to move things aside. He saw shoes, shirts, jackets, and jeans. Stepping back into the bedroom, Macleod pulled open the other drawers. He saw the Captain about to enter and Macleod signalled him to stay back outside.

From down below, there sounded a commotion, and the Captain disappeared quickly down the small set of stairs to the stateroom. The doctor and Macleod quickly followed. A woman had raced in.

'It wouldn't be suicide. He wouldn't kill himself. He wouldn't kill himself.'

'Doctor,' said the Captain, and the doctor walked forward, taking the woman by the hand. He escorted her out of the room, and the Captain watched closely until the door was shut again. He turned to Macleod, but Macleod spoke first.

'That's his wife, or partner. I noticed her by the pool when your third officer took her, informed her, and took her away. Best if she doesn't come back in here until we've taken the photographs and, in fact, you need to seal this cabin. You'll need to get her some clothes and somewhere else to sleep.'

'Of course, Inspector, it's his wife. But I was thinking it's suicide.'

'I like to keep an open mind,' said Macleod. 'I don't come into places deciding straight away what's happened, but I do have numerous years of experience behind me. When I first entered that room, it bothered me. Did he have enough strength to fix the tie that tight around his neck, that close to the fan, and tight enough that it would end up causing him to swing?

'His feet were just about clear of the bed, but he'd still have to pull himself up. It's probably not the easiest place to commit suicide in. You would stand on the bed, and if you didn't get that knot tight enough, or you didn't use the right length of the tie, your feet would hit the bed. You would fail badly at trying to kill yourself,' said Macleod. 'That tells me that somebody worked hard to get that tie precisely correct. The doctor says he can't confirm that the tie asphyxiated the man. He certainly didn't break his neck jumping. He hasn't got the distance to do that.'

'So, what are you saying?' asked the Captain. 'Do you think it was murder?'

'Yes, I think it was murder, or at least, I certainly don't think he committed suicide, and for one overriding reason.'

'And what would that be?' asked the Captain.

'The man doesn't own any ties. None whatsoever. Some-body brought this man a tie or somebody was wearing it when he killed him. I'm sorry, Captain, I think this is murder, and I'm going to need to investigate further.'

Chapter 04

M acleod asked for the room to be sealed and for one person only to enter with a camera. He waited outside the door until the Third Officer arrived.

'Melanie,' said Macleod, 'I take it you're going to be doing the photography.'

'Yes,' she said.

'Disturb nothing. Take photographs from all angles. Make sure that you can see everything within here. Go in on your own and work through it methodically. Go from different angles. We want to be able to see that entire room. Include the ceiling and the floors in that. Photograph the balcony. Photograph access to the balcony from above, below, and from the side,' said Macleod.

'I'd also like you to photograph what's in the drawers. Make sure your hands are gloved so that you don't contaminate or print anything. We'll also get a sample of your hair to get your DNA and send that off just in case we have to look at that at a later date. In truth, it's going to be awkward because obviously people arrived and took the man down, so it seems pretty contaminated. However, I would like a photographic record to send to my team.'

'Of course,' said Melanie. She disappeared and came back with some gloves of the latex variety. Macleod, happy that she'd been briefed correctly and seemed to understand his request, departed back towards the bridge.

The Captain welcomed him again and when asked if Macleod could speak to Mrs Kilmartin, the Captain dispatched Macleod along with one of his officers to find her lying in bed in the medical facilities.

'Macleod,' Dr Felix said, shaking his hand.

'Mrs Kilmartin, is she available to be interviewed?'

'I've calmed her down and I've given her a bit of a sedative,' said the doctor. 'She's obviously distraught, but she's not unwell. In a bit of shock and, yes, by all means, speak to her. If she becomes extremely agitated, please stop.'

'Of course,' said Macleod. 'Don't worry, I've had many years dealing with suspects and, regrettably, many years dealing with grieving relatives. We do try to be sensitive.'

'Of course,' said the doctor. 'If you don't mind, I'll listen in.'

'Of course. Can I ask you just before we do that where you were around the time of the man's death?'

'I've been down in the Medical Centre for the last six hours. I've seen many patients. You can look through the records if you will. You can talk to those patients. I have a full list of them.'

'Excellent,' said Macleod. 'You can sit in then.'

Macleod approached Mrs Kilmartin, taking a seat and placing it beside the bed. She looked over at him, her eyes staring.

'Who might you be?' she asked. He was still in his black trunks and short-sleeve shirt even if it was done up. Macleod thought the question was extremely valid.

'I'm Detective Chief Inspector Macleod, and I work out of Inverness for Police Scotland. It just so happens that I'm on this cruise. I've been asked by the Captain of the boat to investigate what happened to your husband. I'd like to ask you a few questions if you feel up to it. First, let me say I'm sorry for your loss.'

The woman nodded and then lay back, her head hitting the pillow.

'It's been quite a shock, Inspector, but, of course, I'll try.'

'I believe his name was William Kilmartin.'

'Yes, I'm Sandy,' she said. 'I'm his wife and I know what you're probably thinking.'

Macleod gave an expression of bemusement, but he knew what was coming. The woman looked twenty years younger than her deceased husband. She was extremely attractive, and he was wondering was she a trophy wife.

'I am—well, yes. I was Warren's plaything. Warren owned a large sports clothing company. He had a lot of money. I had a lot of dreams about a lifestyle. Don't get me wrong; we have been good for each other, but we both know that we don't really have a lot of love. That being said, it's been a shock. You get used to people about, doing things together.

'Warren was a really nice guy. He did lots of charity work. Even with me, he never treated me like his plaything, his object. Now he was delighted to have me. He enjoyed me being on his arm at certain events. Did he show me off? Yes, but not in a nasty way. He was justly proud of me. Proud of who I was. We had little in common, but it didn't matter. I got what I wanted, and he got what he wanted. We were happy and Warren was well-liked. He's a decent man. Sorry, he was a decent man.' She paused. Macleod saw tears fall.

'Why are you on the cruise?' asked Macleod.

'Warren suggested I needed to relax. He said this was the thing to do. Our cabin's one of the most expensive. It was a thing for him we're not sitting near the casual sort of punter.'

The woman stopped, looked at Macleod and then cried.

'It's all right, just take your time,' said Macleod.

'You're on the vessel too, aren't you? You've not just been flown. Actually, on holiday.'

'Yes,' said Macleod, 'I am one of those punters down below, but it's okay. I don't take offence. We all like to be away from others.'

A part of him wanted to say snob, but he couldn't do it. After all, the woman had lost her husband.

'Your husband died any time between an hour or four hours ago. When did you last see him?'

'I left him this morning to go out to the swimming pool.'

'I saw you there,' said Macleod. 'And your husband was alive when you left him?'

'He wanted to do some work. There's a study. I don't know if you've seen it yet?'

'Up by the bedroom. I glimpsed it.'

'Well, when you own your company, you don't get away with not checking in. He would do that now and then. Usually in the morning and I'd pop off and get a massage, or just have a relaxing time by the pool. I got out of his hair because he was working.'

'Did you leave the door open?' Macleod asked. 'The balcony door was open. It was slightly damp on the inside, on the floor.'

'I didn't. That would be cold. I wouldn't do that. In truth, I was getting out of the way because when Warren talked shop, I didn't like it. He could be very snappy with some people, but

31

he knows what he's doing. He runs the company well, and he earns a lot of money.'

'I noticed that Mr Kilmartin didn't have any ties.'

'No, no. He likes nothing about his neck. Paranoid. Growing up, having to wear a shirt and tie and it got caught one day, and ever since then, he didn't want it. That's what he told me. I remember because I bought him a tie once not long after we were married, and I ended up having to give it away. He'd got incensed and then he said it wasn't my fault because I didn't know.'

She started crying again. 'You think he was murdered?' asked the woman.

'What do you think?' retorted Macleod.

'I told you in the cabin. I said when I came in, I said no. He wouldn't have killed himself. He's too clever, too good at getting out of situations. He's faced rough things before. There were no financial worries. There's no reason for him to kill himself. We're doing well. Him and I are doing well together.'

'Do you know of anyone who would want to kill him?' asked Macleod.

'I've been trying to think,' she said, 'but I don't. That's the thing. He does his charity work. He's a decent man. Yes, he's a businessman. He's got a business head, but actually behind it, he's a big softy.'

'Do you know anyone else on board?'

'Oh, no. No. No. We kept ourselves to ourselves. We actually dine away from other people. There's a rather exclusive restaurant. I don't know if you've seen it.'

Macleod shook his head. He'd heard about it, but there was extra to pay to be in there and it didn't come as part of

Macleod's package on the cruise.

'You probably think I'm a bit of a snob. I just wanted privacy. We could dine together there. Not at the other places. You dine on an enormous table.'

'You don't have to explain yourself,' said Macleod. 'What you do on a cruise is of no concern to me unless it affects your husband's death. Where you dine, I'm struggling to see as part of that. At any point, however, have you or your husband seen anyone here you thought you might have known?'

'No. We've kept ourselves to ourselves. We saw a show one night. He's been to the casino once or twice, but most of the time we spent dining, maybe taking a walk up on the deck, or else just on the balcony. We get a lot of service to the room.'

'How was your husband health-wise?' asked Macleod.

'Perfectly well, as far as I knew.'

'Can you get me the records?' Macleod said to the doctor. 'Just general. Just to make sure he wasn't suffering from cancer or anything. Anything that would give him an excuse to commit suicide.'

'I'll do my best,' said the doctor.

Macleod sat and listened to the early days of the voyage but picked up nothing else from Sandy Kilmartin. The woman seemed in genuine distress. Macleod's mind was made up. The man had been murdered. He didn't know who by. He didn't know why. This said murder to Macleod.

Macleod thanked the woman and then returned to the bridge where he met the Captain. The Captain took him into his ready room at the side. Having closed the door, he asked Macleod to sit down.

'Seoras, are you still of your initial impression that this is murder?'

'I think it's murder,' he said. 'The thing is, how many people do you have on board?'

'Over two thousand passengers,' said the Captain.

'Exactly. We have over two thousand people on board and at the moment, I don't have a single person who's more of a suspect than anyone else. Mrs Kilmartin, if she killed him, is putting on an incredible show.'

'We're on a British vessel,' said the Captain, 'and I have a prerogative that I can investigate. However, I have no experience. You're a law officer from the UK and therefore, I'd like you to investigate.'

'What do you intend to do in the meantime while I'm investigating?'

'What do you mean?'

'You've got over two thousand people on a boat in the middle of nowhere. We're at our next port in three days. The last port is a day behind us. Where do you intend going?'

'I intend to keep to the schedule,' said the Captain. 'It's not unusual we have people die, although to be murdered is certainly unusual. We can keep the body quietly out of the way. I can even keep that cabin locked up for you until you can get forensic people in. Until then, we'll continue with our cruise.'

'Very good,' said Macleod. 'If I'm going to investigate, I'm going to need some more space.'

'Very good,' said the Captain. 'I'll get you a much more suitable cabin. You'll have a stateroom with one study on the side. We've got one free at the moment, wasn't taken for this part of the voyage. We'll upgrade you, your meals, everything. You'll have access to my communications hub. Send anything back and forward. You can explain what you need to keep private and what you don't. As Captain of the vessel, I expect you will report your findings to me. However, I do not wish to get in your way. I can also provide members of the crew to assist. Maybe you'd like someone to accompany you.'

'That's very generous, Captain, but there's only one person who's going to assist me that closely. That'll be Jane, my partner.'

'Is she a police officer as well?' asked the Captain.

'No,' said Macleod. 'I have over two thousand people who are suspects. The one person I know who didn't commit this murder is Jane. Everybody else is as much a suspect as the other. Because of that, I must treat them as such. I won't routinely put evidence in front of you. However, I will keep you briefed and I will advise you on what I'm doing.

'I'll also need to ask you questions at some point, but I think we should keep it relatively quiet. Because of where it happened, I doubt we'll get anyone coming forward to say something was wrong or that they've seen anything. It happened inside a cabin up in the bedroom. I would suspect that anyone up around that area would have reported any loud shouts. However, you'll have to explain why someone is dead. Just say there's been a tragic incident and ask those around if they heard or saw anything. That way, they won't see it as a murder. We'll keep Mrs Kilmartin away from the area, but I think the doctor will want to keep her under observation for a while.'

'Very good,' said the Captain. 'What are you going to do first?'

'The first thing I'm going to do is to get out of these trunks and this shirt. If I'm going to investigate, I will not look like a tourist while I do it.'

'The second thing you'll do?'

'The second bit's a bit more tricky,' said Seoras. 'I'm going to have to go back and convince Jane that she's the perfect investigating partner for me. She wanted a quiet holiday. It looks like Mr Kilmartin's put the kibosh right up that one.'

Chapter 05

'Of all the ships out in all the oceans, we have to get a murdered body in ours. Why this one? Why this boat? Should I have put a clause in? By the way, we don't want to be disturbed. We don't want a busman's holiday. We're not here to get involved in anything.'

'It's not my fault,' said Macleod. 'It's there. It's happened. There's nobody else. The Captain said he looked around. The only other people he's got are a couple of constable-level police officers and they're from foreign countries. It's a British boat.'

'If I'd have booked this on some Portuguese, Spanish, or some other boat, then we would have been fine? They wouldn't have hauled you in?' said Jane.

'Something to do with what's allowed by the UK. I could have investigated but it's a British boat, so it's got to be a British investigation, I think. Anyway, I'm just starting to investigate but that all paperwork will come later.'

'Do people know you're investigating?' asked Jane.

'Some of the crew do. We're not telling everyone that there's been a body found. We're not discussing whether it was murder, suicide, or whatever. Obviously, we can say there are investigations continuing but we're not making a big deal of it. There's over two thousand passengers on this boat, Jane. That's two thousand suspects, and then there's the crew as well . Speaking of which, I need you to accompany me.'

'What? No, no,' said Jane. 'We came away for a holiday. You want to jump in and play detective, then that's up to you. I am going to play person sunbathing at the pool. Possibly even person in the casino.' Macleod glared at her. He knew she said that just to wind him up. 'Yes, I'll be there, and you can give me the money to go.'

'You're not going into the casino,' said Macleod. 'You're going to accompany me.'

'Why on earth would I accompany you when you're running around looking for a murderer? You know that bit where you go to work in the day? I don't follow you; don't go in with you. I'm quite happy not being involved.'

'Difference is this time I need you,' said Macleod.

'I'm not on the payroll,' said Jane. 'Hope, Ross, Clarissa, all those people get paid. How are you going to pay me out here?'

'You're not listening,' said Macleod. 'I need you. There's over two thousand passengers on this ship and I don't know them from Adam. Any of them could have done this except you.'

'What do you mean except me?'

'You were with me all the time,' said Macleod. 'There's no way you could have done it.'

Jane suddenly stopped what she was doing, stood upright with her hands on her hips.

'Really? That's it? I was with you all the time; therefore, I couldn't have done it. Outside of that, no problem at all. Old Jane here could just bump people off left, right, and centre? Thank goodness you were with me, Seoras.'

'That's not what I meant. It's just police speak. It's just the way we look at things. Of course, you wouldn't have done it and if you had, you'd have been much more sensible about it.'

'I wouldn't have been sensible about it at all. I wouldn't have gone near it. Besides, what am I going to do for you?'

'I need someone I can trust, someone to talk to about the case, someone to work with. Normally, I have Hope. On a rare occasion, I'll have Clarissa. Even Ross at times. We don't work on our own. We work with each other, validating what each other is saying. It's how we make sure that we're on the right track. We come up with ideas.'

'They're trained police officers,' said Jane.

'Yes,' said Macleod. 'But this is you. You're not stupid. You know people. I will get a sensible comment out of you. You'll tell me if I'm losing it. I know you're not police. I know you will not be Hope or Ross—or heaven help me, Clarissa. You will be Jane. The person I can talk to. You will ask sensible questions. That's the way you are. For all the feisty little firecracker that I love, you are sensible and will get things done.'

'Feisty little firecracker?' queried Jane. She walked past Macleod as if she was heading into the toilet of their cabin. Then she stopped and wrapped her arms around him from behind. 'Are you sure you want to take on the feisty little firecracker?'

'Oh, they're going to upgrade our cabin as well. We're going up to those up the top.'

'What?' said Jane. 'Really? The stateroom ones? I couldn't afford them. I would have loved those, but I couldn't afford them.'

'It's all right. You don't have to afford it. Captain's giving it to us since I'm doing him a favour.'

'Well, what do we do first?' asked Jane, suddenly warmed to

the idea of helping the investigation.

'I need to call a conference with the Captain and the doctor. We need to sit and go through what's actually happened and then we need a plan of attack. I'll also contact the office after that. See what I can get them doing for me. If we get packed up quick, we can get shifted up towards the new cabin.'

'What's in this cabin, then?'

'It's just a big stateroom. It's got sofas and that. We've got a double bed upstairs.'

'Upstairs? That's not a cabin. It's a small house.'

'There's also a study upstairs,' said Macleod.

'You'll be using that. That's why the Captain's really giving you this, so you've got space to work out of.'

'Look,' said Macleod, 'if I can get on to this quick, get this solved, we can spend the rest of the holiday up in that cabin. We may even push for another week. You don't know what I can get after helping with this.'

'Don't start that trying to make out that you're doing this because it somehow helps me have a big holiday. You're doing this because there's a body out there and somebody's killed that man. Your inner sense, every bit of fibre in your body is going, "Let's get whoever did it." Be honest with me.'

'Yes,' said Macleod. 'That's it exactly. That's me, who I am. You know that.'

'Good. At least we all know that now. Now let's get on.'

Macleod and Jane quickly packed their bags, which were then taken upstairs to the staterooms on the upper decks. Jane strode into the stateroom, admiring it, before walking out to the large balcony. They had one in their previous cabin, but it had been so small by comparison. You could walk along this one, not simply take a couple of steps.

'Wow,' she said, 'Seoras, come and look at this.' Macleod stepped out of the balcony doors.

'What?' he said.

'Just look at this.'

'It's the sea. It's the same sea we saw from down on the other balcony.'

'Seoras Macleod, quit it. Okay? You want me on this investigation with you, you pay lip service at the very least to me.'

'Beautiful view,' said Macleod, walking back inside without even looking. Jane gave a tut to the air. After settling in for half an hour, Macleod and Jane visited the Captain's ready room next to the bridge. He sat behind a desk but had put chairs out and provided tea and coffee for them. The doctor arrived presently, and the four sat down to discuss the case.

'I've tried to have a further examination of the man without causing too much interference,' said the doctor. 'He'd been dead for about two to three hours.'

'His wife had only left three before,' said Macleod. 'That tallies.'

'I'm not sure if when he was hanged if he was conscious or unconscious. He may have been dead when he was hanged. There are lots of markings around the neck.'

'Are they consistent with the tie that was used to hang him up?' asked Macleod.

'I don't know. I can't tell the difference between that and a powerful arm causing massive pressure around the neck. It's not my field. I've taken photographs and if you introduce me to your forensic team, I'll start liaising,' said the doctor. 'I'm sorry I can't give you more, but it's really not my field.'

'It's okay. You'll become the hands and the eyes of my team,' said Macleod. 'I want that body stored and secured. I want it protected,' Macleod said to the Captain. 'That body has to be put away and not interfered with. Doctor, I want you to record exactly what you have done with the body so far. What happened to it? Where it was moved? I want that sent to me in an email.

'I would like you, Captain, to make a note of all the actions that have been taken so far by your crew regarding that cabin. An evidence trail as best we can. I appreciate we're not running with the full efforts of the police force here. We'll do what we can to the best of our ability, and I will get you help for whatever you need. We're a bit out on the time zones, but I should be able to talk to them after this meeting. I would suggest that we head for a port immediately,' said Macleod.

'Why?' asked the Captain.

'We have a murderer on board.'

'If we dock,' said the Captain, 'we'll still have a murderer on board unless we let people off, in which case you will have a murderer who's legged it. I don't see how it's going to help.'

'A murderer off the ship is better than a murderer on. What if he feels under pressure here? What if he feels cornered?' said Macleod. 'I'm not just here to solve the case, I'm here to protect the public, or in this case, your passengers.'

'The company wouldn't wear it.'

'I thought you were responsible.'

'I am responsible for the crew and the passengers and their safety. However, who's to say that any of the other passengers are under threat? Who's to say by going to a port, they will not be under threat? We know nothing. If we turn the ship away, the passengers will want to know why. They'll then panic. I thought part of our idea was to keep this under wraps.'

'That's true, Seoras,' said Jane.

Macleod stood for a moment, thinking. Then he sat down again. 'Okay, but if we catch someone, we have to make an impromptu brig somewhere they can't get out of.'

'We'll do that,' said the Captain. 'In the meantime, I suggest we continue for our next port. We'll be another three days at sea.'

'One thing that bothers me,' said Macleod. 'How easy this seems to have been done. Nobody heard, nobody saw. That means that the victim either knew him or let him in.'

'Let me stop you there,' said the Captain. 'When the door is opened from the interior, it's displayed. Obviously, we don't know who opens it, but it must have been somebody on the inside. However, when it's opened from the outside, it's the key card. We know exactly who's opened it, or rather, which key card. What I can tell you is the door was not opened by key card or by someone from inside.'

'Is there any other way to get in?' asked Jane. 'Any secret panels? Any . . .'

'I'm sorry, Mrs Macleod, but . . .'

'I'm not Mrs Macleod,' said Jane. 'You can just call me Jane. I'm Seoras's partner.'

The Captain nodded his head in apology. 'Jane, this is a vessel. We don't have secret entrances into compartments and cabins. Leaves it far too open to accusations of theft by the crew and also costs a fortune in design. It's straightforward. Your cabin. It's very secure and you go in and out.'

'The door was open,' said Macleod.

'No,' said the Captain. 'The door didn't open. I told you that.'

'The balcony door,' said Macleod.

'We're sailing,' said the Captain. 'You're telling me somebody's crawling along my vessel while we're sailing?'

'I'm not telling you anything,' said Macleod. 'What I know is that the balcony door was open and there was a slightly wet patch. What that means, I don't know, but there's access there. You're telling me from the records that there's no other access made. How secure are those records?'

'That's a good question, Seoras,' said Jane. 'Indeed, how secure are those records?'

Macleod heard the echo. He hoped Jane would be less obvious, stating what he already knew. Of course, it was a good question. He was a detective chief inspector. Macleod was meant to ask the good questions. He was meant to pick up what wasn't being asked. He didn't need a rallying call from her. Macleod caught himself. She didn't need to be put down for trying to help.

'As far as I'm aware,' said the Captain, 'no one can change the records. What is, is what is.'

'I'll need you to give me the type of system that's running and all the details about it. I have a man who can tell me whether what you've just said is true or not.'

'Do you not trust me?' asked the Captain.

'Honestly, I trust you as a person, but you didn't seem very sure of that computer system, so I want that checked out.'

'What do we do first?' asked Jane.

'Well, the Captain and the doctor here have got jobs to do, which we've just discussed. You and I are going to talk to the station. Get a bit of help. I'll make sure the forensic team contact you, doctor. Please avail yourself of every opportunity with them. I take it your colleagues can cover you at the medical centre.'

'They will do,' said the Captain before he could answer.

'In fact, you'll get every bit of help from me that's possible. I've never had someone murdered on my vessel and would rightly like to find those who did it. I'm telling you, the idea of someone coming in from the outside, it doesn't wash with me.'

'It's early days,' said Macleod. 'We have to look at everything.'

Macleod stood up, shook hands with the Captain and the doctor, and exited the little room with Jane, making his way back to their new cabin. Once inside, Jane tapped him on the shoulder.

'Seoras, have you got doubts about the Captain?'

'No,' he said. 'Not at all. No doubts about the doctor either. In fact, they're going to be the easiest ones to watch. The idea that a Captain would bump someone off, why? On his own voyage. He'd have to investigate. Why would he ask me to come in? The Captain is not involved in this. We just need to make sure that he or his people don't blow a key bit of evidence.

'I also like the idea of everybody being off this boat before the murderer can do anything else. What we do in solving murders is protect people. Sometimes you have to protect them first rather than find out who killed the dead.'

'What about no one coming through the stateroom door?'

'It's a possibility, but I'm very untrustworthy about computers. I need to talk to Hope and Ross—find out what's going on.' With that, he traipsed up the stairs to the study.

'Do you want me here or not?' asked Jane.

'It'll bore the pants off you. If you're really interested, of course you can come. Otherwise, no. Forget it.'

'That's fine,' said Jane. 'It's time for a cup of tea.'

Chapter 06

Hope McGrath hung her jacket up on the coat stand before turning and walking over to her desk. She looked out the window and then stopped, smiling to herself. No Macleod to bother her today. No proper cases on the go and a slightly late arrival because she'd woke up early this morning. And then she'd woken John up.

She was feeling good. It had been her idea, after all. She'd be getting home late from the office, often so tired. John was also tired, and ultimately, they ended up just falling asleep. They weren't some old married couple, and Hope wanted a little more life in the relationship than that. She had resolved to start the day off with something for her and John. Admittedly, she was going to get up and make croissants, but when she saw him lying there, she couldn't help herself and now she had skipped into the building.

Her smile broke as the phone rang. It was the switchboard operator sending a call through. Hope was advised that there was a call routing in from a vessel in some ocean.

'You have advised them I cover the Highlands and Islands,' said Hope, laughing to the switchboard operator.

'It's okay. The man on the communications set from the

vessel said that you know who's calling.'

That stopped Hope for a moment. *Why would he do that? Why would he call her up? He's on holiday. I'm fine. I know I can do this job, it's not a problem. Sod off, Seoras,'* thought Hope.

'Hello,' came the voice at the other end. 'Is that you, Hope?'

'Seoras, to what do I owe this pleasure? I thought you were on holiday.'

'I thought I was on holiday as well, but I've got a body on the boat.'

Hope should have said, 'That's terrible. How can I help?' instead, she burst out laughing.

'I'm not joking,' said Macleod. 'Somebody's been murdered on this boat. I've got a suspect list of a couple of thousand.'

'Who's dealing with it?'

'I am,' said Macleod. 'British vessel. They're looking for somebody British to investigate. I'm the only British police officer there is, so I'm doing it and you lot are getting co-opted to give me a hand.'

'I'll go pack my bags,' said Hope.

'No, you're staying where you are. I said you're getting co-opted; I didn't say you're being flown out.'

'Well, that's hardly fair.'

'I didn't say it was fair. The thing is, I've got nothing out here. It's just me and Jane.'

'How is she? Is she going to be okay relaxing on her own?' asked Hope.

'She is going to help me,' said Macleod.

'You can't do that. Jane's a civilian.'

'She'll remain a civilian. I said she was going to help me. I didn't say she was going to arrest people.'

'Are you sure about this, Seoras?'

'Well, I haven't got you, have I?'

'Since when did you need me?' asked Hope.

'I've always needed you. You've always needed Ross. Ross always needs Cunningham. Clarissa needs Patterson. Patterson needs somebody from I don't know where. It's the team. We work, we bounce off each other. You're a DI now and you don't know this?'

'I didn't talk about other people—I said you. You never really needed me, did you? Only for the legwork.'

'That's not true,' said Macleod. 'You spark things in my head. You challenge what I'm thinking. Of course, I need you and I haven't got you, so I've got Jane.'

'What did you tell her?'

'I told her she was the only one I could trust because there's two thousand plus other suspects.'

'That would have gone down really well,' said Hope. 'You need me. You need me to stop your relationship from falling apart with comments like that.'

'She's on board that you're on board. Right, the person who died—have you got a pen?'

'Got a pen. Of course, I've got a pen,' said Hope. 'I'm a police officer.'

'Write,' said Macleod. As he spoke, Hope realised she didn't have a pen and was scrambling along her desk to find one. By the time she grabbed one, he was already halfway through his sentence.

'Warren Kilmartin is the dead man,' he said. 'Owner of a large sports clothing company. Get Ross onto it. I want every detail about the man. Sandy Kilmartin's the wife. She's twenty years younger. She's a bit of a looker, but I doubt it's a pristine marriage. They say they get along, but who knows? They're the only two people we've got who we know are involved. One, him because he's dead, and two, her, because she went out before he died. Tell Ross I want everything he can find. Any dirt, any people attached to him.'

'Of course,' said Hope. 'Anything else?'

'I'll give you the ship's number. We're going to need Jona to tell a doctor how to look after evidence and a body. His name's Dr Felix. I'll give you the communications room for the ship. Get Jona to contact them. Unfortunately, they found the man hanging from a fan in a bedroom. They took him down to save his life, but he was already dead, so the room's pretty contaminated. The doctor is unsure if the tie around the man's neck killed him. Said he hasn't got the skills. I've had the entire room photographed from all angles, and I'll be firing them across to you so you guys can look at it. Have you got anything running now at home?'

'It's fairly quiet,' said Hope.

'Good,' said Macleod. 'You have plenty of time then to get on to this for me. Give me a buzz when you've sorted something out. I've emailed the doctor's report over and the scene's photos.'

'Is the Captain aware of who he's actually got involved in this?'

'Don't start,' said Macleod. 'This is my holiday, too. I haven't just ditched it for a laugh.'

'I bet Jane's right happy about it.'

'Shut up, Hope,' said Macleod. 'Get me all the information, and then get back to me.'

Macleod came down from the study to find Jane, who made him a cup of coffee. It was instant, and not good. Macleod drank it and then asked quickly afterwards if Jane fancied something to drink. She wasn't even three-quarters of the way through her cup of tea.

Macleod took a long route around the vessel, dropping into the Captain to ask for ship schematics, and then walking by the coffee shop on the main promenade. He sat down with Jane, a rather sombre face on.

'I normally keep you well out of these things and I'm sorry to bring you in.'

'It is what it is, Seoras. What's the pep talk for?'

'We're looking to chase down a murderer, potentially. Stay close. Don't go anywhere on your own, don't get lost on your own. If anything happens around you, shout.'

'Do you tell that to all your officers?'

'No, my officers are trained to deal with themselves and to deal with attackers. You're not. You haven't got a clue.'

'No, I haven't,' said Jane.

'That's fine because I'm not bringing you in for your fighting abilities,' said Macleod. 'I'm looking for someone to challenge what I say and bring her own ideas.'

'You've got the ship schematics. Why?'

'Well,' said Macleod, 'one thing you mentioned was about that the door being opened. Can somebody get in from the outside balcony? Well, I've got the schematics, we're going to have a have a look at it, then we're going to visit the computer systems. I need to remind the Captain to send that detail off to Ross.'

Macleod and Jane spent the next hour and a half walking around the vessel. They pinpointed where the cabin was, and from below and from above, they looked to see how you would access the balcony.

'If you ask me, you could get there. You'd need somebody

up this end to hang on to things or you'd need to fix your line. But you could get down, I'm sure of it,' said Jane.

Macleod looked down at the side of the vessel. 'Are you sure? Because I sure wouldn't want to be doing that.'

'Seoras, you don't even play football or anything. You see golf as an over-exercise. Come on. It isn't you doing this, is it? It's going to be somebody with a bit of skill.'

'It'd need to be a climber,' said Macleod.

'Actually, it'd probably help to know how to operate the ropes and that. He could, of course, be a proper hitman, couldn't he?'

'No,' said Macleod.

'What do you mean, no?'

'A hitman wouldn't choose here. Why would a hitman choose here? Nowhere to go. You would also make sure the person was dead. And why would you hang them up like it was a suicide? A hitman hits. This is somebody who wanted it not to be recognised for what it was. It's not a hitman. A hitman wants to make sure that you pay him, so he points out the fact that the person was killed, not that they committed suicide.'

'If you could get in, though, you'd also have to get out. Have access points,' said Jane. 'You'd have to know I'm going from here to here because I guess it'd be quite scary on the outside there. It certainly gives me the heebie-jeebies. Are we going to have a look at the computer system?'

Macleod nodded. The pair walked back to the bridge when the Captain escorted them off to see the computer systems which showed the access to all the cabins.

'If you look at the timings when the door opens, that's what, about three hours beforehand, before when he's been found?

51

That'll be Mrs Kilmartin coming out.'

'Can't she just push the door open and then let it close? There's no proof she's actually walked out, is there?' asked Jane.

'The system shows the door opening. Whether somebody went through it, we don't know,' said the operator who had been posted with the pair of them. The Captain was staying back, seemingly wary of Macleod's and Jane's questions.

'According to your system,' said Macleod, 'that room was not accessed at all.'

'No, there's a possibility that the room was departed from three hours before because the door was open.'

'Or somebody came in. Maybe his wife has a fancy man, and he came in and did the deed, swapped around.'

'How does he get out afterwards?' asked Macleod. 'He then what, jumps out the side? I'd imagine you could go from the outside in. Of course. he could have run out when she came back, but no one saw anyone.'

'You'd have to climb up, though. That's a tough climb,' said the Captain from behind her. 'With the boat at sea, it's difficult. Much easier to come down than go up.'

'Did you get the specs from the computer assistant, please?' asked Macleod to the Captain. The man nodded and Macleod took him over to the terminal so he could email Ross with all the information. When he'd done so and Macleod had looked through the records, Jane and he returned to the coffeehouse of earlier.

'Where are we at?' Jane asked.

'Early days,' said Macleod. 'At the moment, we have got no suspects. We have got no reason for his wife to kill him. More than that, I've actually met her, and you don't fool me very often,' said Macleod. 'I haven't got evidence to eliminate her, but I have got nothing to incriminate either. Other than that, we've got the other two thousand passengers.'

'Should we interview them?'

'We've got three days before this boat arrives in port,' said Macleod. 'You want to interview them all? It'll be like a three-second interview to keep them moving.'

'You're saying to me that's not an idea?'

'We need to make a breakthrough and make it quick if we're going to catch this killer. Otherwise, he could just lie low and get off the boat,' said Macleod.

'The computer systems aren't often wrong,' said Jane. 'I know you're wary of them because you think data can always be manipulated, but it doesn't happen that often, does it?'

Macleod nodded. She was right.

'Because of that,' said Jane, 'I think he's coming in through the balcony door.'

'What's the wet patch for?' said Macleod. 'That makes little sense. Why is there a wet patch?'

'Depends on what it was wet from.'

When they finished their coffee, Macleod took Jane up to the top deck, looking down towards where the cabin had been infiltrated. There wasn't a lot of places to come from above. After all, the cabin was nearly on the top deck. Macleod looked down. 'How rough was the spray?'

'This morning,' said Jane, 'it was pretty bad.'

'If he came from below, you might get soaked. You might deposit some water,' said Macleod.

'How do we know, though?' asked Jane.

'Well, we don't,' said Macleod. 'We've got to make some educated guesses on the way here, but if you're coming up

53

from below, you've got to have somewhere to go to. I think this is something we should look at.'

'Does it always go like this?' asked Jane. 'It seems to me that we don't have a lot and there's not an awful lot to be gained from the little things.'

'The early part of the investigation is poking around with a stick in the dark,' said Macleod. 'When things emerge, you put them together and you see where you can go with them. At the moment, we're stuck because we need a bit more information. My hunch is on the computer systems. Yours is on somebody coming from the outside. We'll have to see what we can dig up.

'We also need to know about Warren Kilmartin. I need to find out what he was like as the wealthy owner of a business. We presume the wife was getting the inheritance, which means,' said Macleod, 'that either she's greedy as anything or someone else is benefiting in some way.

'Just one more thing,' continued Macleod, and he sneaked an arm around her back. 'Don't put any distance between you and me. Make sure you stay close at all times. The last time on a case when I went off the boil . . .'

'Hope ended up scarred,' said Jane. 'I know and I know that bites. She saved me that day.'

'Just remember, in all the fun and the excitement of solving the case, we've got a killer on the loose. The last thing I need is for you to get in his way.'

'At last,' said Jane, 'you finally know how I feel.'

Chapter 07

'Seoras, would you get out of that shower? Ross is on the phone.'

Macleod groaned. He hadn't been in the shower that long, maybe two minutes. The en suite he was now in was far superior to the one he'd had on the lower deck. The shower was reviving, and he wanted to stay there. He'd been disturbed from his holiday, albeit pepping him up with a case to solve, but he also wanted his moments with Jane, and his time alone.

Despite the stateroom, being on board a vessel with so many people still seemed cramped to him. He would rather be in the countryside with no one around and no one to see for miles.

Macleod switched off the shower, stepped out, and dried himself down before wrapping himself up in a gown. He hurried through to the study.

'I've got Ross here,' said Jane, pointing at a screen. Macleod sat down in a chair and Ross waved up at him.

'Sir, sorry to disturb you. You had asked me to have a look at Warren Kilmartin.'

'That I did, and not that long ago. That was quick, Ross.'

'Well, I didn't know when you'd be going to bed. The times are not great.'

'What have you found out?' asked Macleod.

'Well, he started his business twenty years ago, Kilmartin Clothing, and it became Kilmartin Sports. I don't know where he got the collateral to actually start-up. It's not coming through. Nothing obvious. No borrowing, nothing I can run down. I'll keep looking, but that was twenty years ago. He's well-respected in the business world, and he's a bit of a philanthropist. Apparently, he's put money into hospitals, kids' projects, inner cities. He seems a decent guy. He married his wife, Sandy. She was a model he seemed to be interested in, and they had a happy life, and when I say she was a model, she was a glamour model.'

'Oh, she did the fashions and that?' said Jane over Macleod's shoulder.

'No,' said Ross. 'Not that sort of glamour one. Like the ones that used to be in the tabloids.'

'She kept that quiet,' said Jane. 'She said nothing to you about that Seoras, did she, when she was down in the medical centre?'

'No,' said Macleod. 'Her husband had just been killed. It's not the sort of thing you necessarily would mention.'

Jane looked at him and gave a little shake of her head. 'Suppose so.'

'The thing is that she's the direct benefactor of his death,' said Ross. 'The house, the money, the business, all go to her. So, from that point of view, if she didn't like him, she'd certainly be a suspect.'

'But if it's not her,' said Macleod, 'then whoever was doing it wasn't after the money. There was nothing stolen from the cabin either.'

'What does that mean?' said Jane.

'It means it's personal. If it's not Sandy, it's something

personal. Why go kill somebody unless you have a reason? Keep digging into his past, Ross. Did he offend someone? Did he do the dirty on someone in the early days? Keep looking.'

'I will do.'

Macleod closed down the call with Ross and the doorbell of their cabin rang.

'I'll get it,' said Jane. 'You're in no state to be answering doors.' Macleod looked at the towelling robe around him. She was right.

'Oh, hello. The First Officer? Okay. Yes, he'll be available in a minute. He's just had a shower. He's getting changed. I'll tell him and we will be there directly.'

Macleod heard Jane bounce back up the stairs and she met him in the bedroom.

'It's the First Officer. He says he had a passenger come forward to say his cabin was broken into and he believes a tie is missing.'

'What's the passenger's name?'

'Somebody Flowers,' said Jane. 'I didn't quite catch it.'

Macleod was amazed at the information that just went past Jane, but then again, she wasn't trained. Sometimes you only heard things once, and you needed to make sure that they stuck.

'I'll be interviewing the man directly.' Macleod put some pants on, and Jane didn't leave the bedroom. Feeling self-conscious, Macleod stood up.

'What?' he asked.

'All convenient, isn't it? Strange?'

'What do you mean?' asked Macleod.

'Why would you complain about a tie being stolen? Your room being broken into, and somebody stole a tie?'

'Possibly because somebody broke into your room and stole a tie. I mean, it's something to report. They haven't put two and two together that the tie was from a dead man because they won't know. The crew, at least some of the top end of the crew, know, so they'd have referred it to us.'

'Do you think Mrs Kilmartin knew something about it?' asked Jane.

'When I spoke to her, I didn't get that feeling. She seemed distraught. She seemed shocked. You saw her when they gave the news. How did you think she reacted then?'

'Oh, for goodness' sake, Seoras. That was like, how long ago now? I wasn't looking for it. I wasn't . . .'

'I saw it. Her reaction seemed genuine.'

'But that's the thing, isn't it,' said Jane. 'I don't walk around looking for suspects. I don't walk around thinking that somebody might be guilty, so I better watch what they're doing. It just switches on with you, doesn't it? It just clicks. You just happen to see something occurring and the brain goes, "How are they reacting? How are they doing that? She looks guilty. He doesn't. Blah, blah, blah." That's all I get when you go out with me, or we go shopping. You do that too. I've seen you when you watch people. There's almost an accusation at people without opening your mouth.'

'I think that's harsh.'

'It isn't, and you're going to have to listen to it anyway because you're stuck on this case with me.'

The doorbell rang again and Macleod quickly got changed. He raced down to open the door to say he was coming along presently, but the doctor was standing there along with Sandy Kilmartin.

'Hello,' said Macleod. 'How can I help?'

58

'Mrs Kilmartin wanted to know what was happening. I told her I had to do certain checks around her husband's body and she seemed quite anxious about it.'

'There's no need,' said Macleod. 'It's all perfectly routine.'

'But I need to talk to you,' said Sandy Kilmartin.

Macleod ushered her into the room and pointed to the sofa. 'Not in front of the doctor,' she said. 'This is very personal.'

'He's your doctor.'

'He's not my doctor,' she said to Macleod. Macleod turned and gave the doctor a nod and he stepped outside of the room.

'I hope you don't think I'm too forward,' said Sandy Kilmartin. She was dressed in blouse and black trousers. 'I obviously want to assist any way I can, Inspector, but I really could do without all of this hassle. I don't know if I can make things run any smoother.'

Macleod watched as she unbuttoned her blouse. She got three buttons down before she heard the footsteps coming down the steps.

'Impromptu interview, is it?' asked Jane. 'Well, I'm here. You must be Mrs Kilmartin. You seem to be doing very well. Seoras said you weren't doing great earlier on.' The woman looked flustered, quickly doing up her blouse.

'We got some reports from home. You told Seoras that you were a model, but apparently, you were a glamour model.'

No, she didn't, thought Macleod. *Ross told us. Don't give out what you know.*

'Yes. Not that much difference, is there?'

'Well, no, not to me. I don't look for that sort of thing. What do you think, Seoras? Someone walking down the catwalk, someone on the inside pages of the paper, any difference?' Macleod almost went slightly red.

'Perfectly reasonable occupation.'

'How did you meet your husband?' asked Jane.

'He approached me. He approached me because he said I looked beautiful.'

'And where did he see you? Were you at a catwalk show, at a gala dinner, were you—'

'He saw me in the paper. He called me up.'

'And you accepted a call from a guy just ringing up?' said Macleod.

'Of course. He was loaded.'

'So, you just wanted the money?' asked Jane. 'You just wanted the money. Do you still want the money? Is that what—'

Jane felt a hand go up onto her shoulder and gently tap it.

'What Jane's trying to ask,' said Macleod, 'is what sort of access to his money did he give you? Do you have instant access to it or are you not able to get any of the money? Did he give you an allowance, Mr Kilmartin?'

'Our bank accounts are joint.'

'Or are they?' asked Jane.

'We can check that separately,' said Macleod, in her ear. 'You don't need to follow that line. Let me lead.'

'One problem I have,' said Macleod, 'is you've come here. Before Jane came down those stairs, you were almost offering me something to make everything run smoother. Why? Why do you need it to go smoothly?'

'Because there'll be scandal, won't there? "He's dead. Did she kill him?" I used to be in the papers. I used to be displayed in the papers, you know? And the one thing about papers is that if they can find any smut, they'll plaster it everywhere. I've stepped aside. We've had a good life, mainly thanks to

Warren, and now Warren's gone. I don't want to be thrown out and into the tabloid hell. When I first got with him, they said he was only after one thing. Well, they said two things, but I know what they meant.'

'Trying to influence an officer in the course of his duty,' said Macleod, 'is an extremely unwise thing to do. Doing it in his cabin is even more unwise and doing it within earshot of his partner is possibly foolhardy.'

The woman looked over at Jane, who was smiling. 'You have nothing to fear from me. I am not looking to make a circus of this,' said Macleod. 'I want you to go and to rest up. You didn't do it, Mrs Kilmartin. If I thought you had, I'd have arrested you by now, but you didn't. You were out. I saw the reaction that you gave. Many people can play at things, can act well. You can't, so try nothing. Just let me get on with my business, and I'll clear up everything as quick as I can because I don't want to be in the papers either. I've been there, and it's not good.'

The woman looked quizzically at Macleod before he walked over to the door, opened it, and asked for the doctor to come back in.

'Take Mrs Kilmartin back to her bed, please. She needs to rest up. Look out for emails and contact from my team, doctor. They'll be here shortly.'

The doctor gave a nod and disappeared with Sandy Kilmartin. As Macleod walked back into the room, Jane looked at him. 'She tried to come on to you. Is this normal? Does this happen to you a lot?'

'Do I look like a man who has women come on to him a lot?' said Macleod. 'It's not a good thing either. She's desperate, but she's not the killer. She can't hide things well.'

'How do you know that?' asked Jane.

'Experience. I read people. It's what I do well. Like you; at the moment, you're angry underneath at her. You're a little angry at me, but you're angry at yourself because you shouldn't be angry at me because I dealt with it. You're also annoyed because our holiday's being spoiled, and we can't get on with other things. Yet you know that's not fair to me. Point it in the right direction,' said Macleod. 'Let's go find this killer. The quicker we do it, the quicker we get back to having our holiday. The next thing we've got to do is to go see Flowers.'

'I think it was Flowers; they said It might have been in a slightly foreign accent. It was one of the crew members. They weren't from Britain,' said Jane. 'One of those foreign-type lingos.'

Macleod nodded, and together, the pair exited the room. Macleod wondered what was coming. It seemed strange. One man hanged with a tie, and suddenly somebody's tie was missing. It was almost too smooth, and it begged the question, why? Why on earth would you take somebody else's tie to do it? It was time to find out why.

Macleod took Jane's hand, and they were shown to the cabin of the man reporting his tie as missing. The distance was not far, for it was another one of the more expensive staterooms.

'Good,' said Macleod, standing outside.

'Why good?' asked Jane.

'Posh cabin, tie stolen, man dies in posh cabin. This is operating on a level. Most people on this boat can't afford cabins like this. If people up at this high level are killing each other, then at least they won't be taking out the one thousand, five hundred or so down below.'

'Keep them safe first,' said Jane. 'That's what you said, wasn't it?'

'That's why we do it,' said Macleod. 'Now let's see why someone would nick a tie.'

Chapter 08

Macleod stepped forward into the salubrious cabin, the first officer leading the way. 'Chief Detective Inspector Macleod, this is Professor Carlos Flores.'

Macleod glanced over a shoulder at Jane, who just shook her shoulders. *Flowers indeed.*

'Professor Flores,' said Macleod. 'I hear you've been having a bit of trouble.'

Flores nodded profusely. He was a small man, bald with bushy eyebrows, and seemed to find it hard to focus on anyone. More of an instinctive busyness as opposed to a tick, he would jerk here and there examining this and that with his eyes. For a moment, he looked at Macleod, then at Jane, and back at Macleod.

'Inspector,' he said, 'they took my tie.'

Macleod could see the man was wearing a tie. This one, green and yellow on a brown shirt, looked positively hideous. But Macleod held his tongue while Professor Flores turned around in the room. The cabin was very similar to that of the Kilmartins. Macleod followed Flores over to the outside balcony door.

'This time a day ago, that cabin door was open. That is when the tie was taken.'

'Have we got a photograph?' asked Macleod of the first officer. 'One of the tie?'

The first officer produced a small tablet and whipped through different photographs before handing it to Macleod. Macleod looked and saw the tie that had been used to hang Kilmartin. He turned the tablet round, offering it to Professor Flores.

'Could you just confirm if the tie that was taken had the same design as this one?'

'That's my tie,' said Flores. 'That's my tie.'

'You say you noticed the tie was gone a day ago? Did you report this?'

'Of course, I didn't report it. We've been looking for it. I was trying to get hold of my daughter. She wasn't here. She was out and about. Alessandra,' he shouted. 'Alessandra!'

From the top of the stairs came a shout, 'Father? What?'

'The policeman is here. He needs to speak to you.'

'I'm in my room.'

'Come down here now,' shouted her father indignantly.

Macleod looked up and saw a young woman racing down the stairs. Her legs were bare, and she was wearing a dressing gown over the top of some form of pyjama top and bottoms. The dressing gown was open, and as she arrived at the bottom of the stairs, her father stepped across to her.

'Enough of that,' he grabbed the dressing gown, pulling it across her. 'This is Detective Inspector Macleod.'

'Detective Chief Inspector Macleod,' said Jane from behind Seoras. Seoras turned and looked at her, giving a little shake of the head. He was well used to having his title completely mispronounced. He would not blame a foreigner.

'Your father is saying that one of his ties has been missing. He said it happened a day ago when the door was open.'

'Does he?' said the daughter. 'I don't know. I wasn't here. It's what he told me that day, but I don't know.' Her father looked furious with her.

'Get back up the stairs,' said the professor.

'No, don't,' said Macleod. 'Best if you're both here, sir. Alessandra,' said Macleod, 'if you could sit down, we'll talk to you momentarily. I just want to conclude with your father.'

The professor stared at Alessandra, then his eyes darted back to Macleod, then Jane, then the first officer, and then started moving again. It was extremely unsettling. Macleod felt like he was on some sort of boat as he tried to watch where the eyes were going. Like an insane tennis match, he would just pop from one person to the other.

'Professor, why are you on this cruise, if you don't mind me asking?' said Macleod.

'I am on a family trip,' said Flores.

'Is your wife with you?'

The professor's mood grew dark. 'No,' he said.

'Mother won't travel with him. He's too weird,' said Alessandra. Macleod walked across to her, kneeling down so he was at the same height as she sat on the sofa. Despite her father earlier adjusting her gown, it now sat open again, her bare legs out in front of Macleod.

'Forgive me,' said Macleod, 'but you don't seem to be a magnificent pair together.'

'I am here for fun. He is here for who knows what. I am a twenty-year-old woman. I can happily look after myself.'

Macleod realised Flores spoke with a heavy accent, unlike

Alessandra. If he had heard her voice first, he never would've put her name with her. In fact, he was thinking she was possibly from somewhere near Leeds.

'And what is it you do here?' asked Macleod.

'Enjoy myself. That's why we're all here.'

'Why we're meant to be here,' Macleod heard whispered behind him. It was low enough in volume only Macleod picked it up, but he still didn't appreciate the effort from Jane.

'If you don't mind me asking, did we see you round the pool?'

'I like to sunbathe up in that top corner. It's rather good up there. Quiet, too. The bar is excellent.'

'Pools, bars. You should do some research. You should be at university,' said Flores. 'It's your mother's fault. Your mother has you doing this.'

'Can we hold on a minute?' said Macleod. 'I'm not here to discuss family matters. You say your tie was missing?'

'Yes. A day ago, that door was open. That's when it went missing.'

'When did you discover it missing?' asked Macleod.

'About an hour ago, I went to change. I have nothing else that colour. It's the only thing that went with my shirt.'

'Your shirts,' said Alessandra. 'They're ridiculous. You look like some sort of confectionary clown, the number of colours you have. Why can't you just dress sensibly? Just wear something normal. Something like this man.' Alessandra pointed to Macleod. He was in a normal shirt, was he? Normal trousers? This was as close to work wear as he could get.

'There's something to be said for a bit of colour.'

Not now, Jane, thought Macleod. 'Just to confirm—that's yours. You've gone looking for your tie about an hour ago, and it's not there. Having done this, you did what?'

67

'Reported it. I only just realised it definitely wasn't here. I thought it was missing a day ago. The door was open, so therefore, that's when it must have been taken.'

'You can confirm it was definitely missing a day ago?'

'I think it wasn't on the rack. I have a rack upstairs, the ties, they hang from it.'

'How many ties do you have?' asked Macleod.

'Sixty-four,' said Alessandra.

'Sixty-four?' blurted Jane. 'How long are you on this cruise?'

'A month,' said the girl.

'You're wearing two ties a day?' asked Jane.

'When one wants to look smart.'

'Stop,' said Macleod. 'I'm not here as the fashion police. I'm not here to say what you should or shouldn't wear. I just need to know about this tie,' he said, pointing to the tablet. 'Was it definitely missing a day ago?'

'I assume it was. Can't remember seeing it. I definitely didn't have it an hour or two ago. That's when I reported it. I wanted to check with my daughter. She wasn't here. Then she comes back, and now . . .'

'I have to tell you, said Macleod, 'that a man in a cabin near to here was hanged with that tie.'

'He took my tie to hang himself?'

'That's awful, said Alessandra. 'If he were going to die, he would use a better-looking tie than that one.'

Her father rolled his eyes at her. Macleod just shook his head in disbelief, while Jane couldn't believe the liberty the girl was taking at making such a joke.

'It's no laughing matter,' said Macleod. 'He's dead. Possibly killed with the tie. I'm afraid I'm going to have to talk to you about your movements yesterday.'

'I don't know,' said the professor. 'In and out, at the casino, I think. Dinner, lunch. Oh, I don't know. Something like that.'

'Your movements, Miss Flores?' asked Macleod.

'I—well, it would have been the pool or the gym. I haven't really gone anywhere else. Occasionally, I might go to the bar late at night, but not these last couple of nights.'

'In the evening, you are what?' asked Macleod.

'Up by the pool, the gym.'

Macleod had seen some people up by the pool, but they weren't in it late at night. It was more of a social thing. He'd walked past the last two days, not stopping, but he hadn't noticed Alessandra. She was good-looking with dark eyes and long, black hair. Although not one to particularly focus on women these days, Macleod would have spotted her.

'Did you cash in any money at the casino?' asked Macleod.

'All the time,' said the professor. 'It's not a crime. A man can play.'

'Do you have the money to play?' asked Jane, causing Macleod to give his head a little shake. It was the right question asked in the wrong way. *There are ways and means. We could find out about his bank accounts. We could find out from Ross.*

'My financial state is excellent.'

Macleod looked over at Alessandra. She wasn't laughing. 'He's telling the truth, Inspector. We are well off. That is one thing that my parents have given me: a touch of wealth. Outside of that, absolutely nothing.'

'Get to your room,' said the professor. This time, Macleod let the young women go as she stormed off up the stairs.

'I've got some records to check,' said Macleod. 'Don't go anywhere.'

'We're on a boat,' said Professor Flores. 'Where am I going?'

69

'I'll be in touch,' said Macleod, turning, and he walked outside of the door, followed by Jane and the first officer. When the door closed behind them, he turned to the first officer. 'Do you have any details on the professor, what he was saying there about the casino?'

'I know he's been found in the casino, morning, noon and night. Gambling, spending, never really winning much. His daughter is indeed usually up by the pool or the gym. I know some of the young bartenders have noticed her.'

'Seoras, you should know that she's very like Sandy Kilmartin.'

'I'm sorry?' said Macleod. 'What do you mean?'

'Alessandra, she's very like Sandy Kilmartin, the eyes rove. Some women, they're looking at men all the time. You men do it more often to women. Scanning the crowd, picking out who you really like. A lot of us are well used to that, but women like this, they pick what they want. They're hungry for it. Strange that Sandy Kilmartin's doing that after her husband's died, and the daughter's doing it in front of her father. Clearly not ashamed. I would say that's a woman who would take to sexual action, or at least to form a strong relationship of some sort, however brief it might be.'

'Who is she looking at?' asked Macleod.

'Not you,' said Jane. 'Our first officer here. You look smart enough,' Jane said to him as she saw the shock on his face. 'We've got eyes that rove, too, Seoras. Eyes that rove.'

'What do you know about eyes that rove?' he asked. 'It's not a very—well . . .'

'What?'

'Professional opinion. It's not very . . .'

'Didn't think that mattered,' said Jane. 'He asks for my help,' she said to the first officer, 'then when I'm offering my opinion, he questions it. You can take it or leave it, Mr Detective.'

Macleod left it and turned to the first officer. 'I'll need to go through the door codes again. See who's been in and out of this one. Is there any way to know if that balcony door was open a day ago.'

'We do not know,' said the first officer. 'It's a basic lock from the inside. Hard to get at from the outside.'

'Can you get at it? Can you open it?'

'If you were good,' said the first officer, 'you'd have to know how to. You'd have to probably have lock pick tools with you. It's not electronically tied, as we don't expect anyone to be bursting in from those balconies. They are not the easiest things to access from outside.'

Macleod nodded. 'Get me the logs then,' he said. 'We'll go through them. See who's been in and out. See if the professor has any other friends that come.'

'Oh, no,' said the first officer. 'He's always alone, always gambling.'

'What about Alessandra?' asked Jane. 'Is she always alone?'

'The young men I've asked say that often, but not always.'

'Who's she with?' asked Macleod.

'Men,' said the first officer. 'Jane is correct in her assumption. She may have those eyes that rove.'

Macleod was still not completely sure what was being meant, but he decided not to waste any more time. 'Please get the information on the doors, please,' said Macleod. 'I shall take Jane here for dinner. You can't work on an empty stomach.'

'You've worked on an empty stomach a load of times,' said Jane. 'I had to drop off food to you because you don't eat.'

But Macleod was away, and Jane tore off up the corridor

after him. It was time to eat.

Chapter 09

Sylvia appeared around the edge of the corridor, scanning it to see if anyone was about. The towel hung off her neck. She lifted it up to wipe down her flushed face. She was shaking, trembling, in fact. There was fear there. She'd been seen, after all.

They had been seen in the most uncompromising position. She didn't get to glance at the person who had walked in. It was a woman. She knew from the retreating shape. The door had opened. The woman had half gone to scream and then coughed, almost apologising as she disappeared out the door. Sylvia had gone white and then turned and looked at her lover below her. With a mutual glance, they disengaged from their act and Sylvia began throwing on the clothes that had earlier been discarded. By the time she was changed, her lover was gone.

She was dishevelled, though. Her tracksuit bottoms on, the zipped tracksuit top over the upper half of her body, but nothing underneath. Underwear and t-shirt were stuffed into one pocket on the zipped jacket. She'd grabbed a towel, hung it around her neck to give the impression that the exhausted look was coming from exercise of a more fitness-based regime.

She had to get back to the cabin and slip into the shower before David saw her. He would know. Sylvia was convinced he would know. After all, there were telltale signs, weren't there? When you normally exercised, yes, you were sweating, but what she had been doing, that involved other smells. Her face, which had briefly gone white, had suddenly become exhilarated again. Yes, it was a shock to be caught in the act, but now she felt, well, naughty. Was that the word? Alive?

Life with David was dull. He wasn't a man who paid great attention to his wife. While he was rich enough and had everything they needed, what she didn't have was the companion that she'd sought. Instead, she got a man who liked to drink, liked to be in amongst the crowd and lording it over them, telling them how wonderful he was.

Was she a trophy wife? Not really, but she was pretty convinced he had other trophies. Other women stashed away here and there. If he would not pay her attention, she was going to get it elsewhere. This cruise was going to be one glorious holiday for her, as long as she didn't have people walking in, spying her on the only activity that her husband would probably get rid of her for.

She peeked around the corner of the corridor, Sylvia unzipped slightly, letting the heat from the top of her cleavage escape. She ran her hand across the chain around her neck, fumbling it between her fingers. Her mind drifted back to those moments, drifted back to the excitement. They could have just gone to his cabin, but that wasn't exciting enough. She was like a teenager again, like a young girl experiencing love for the first time. Was it love? More like want and need, her body being let loose.

It was a funny thing, wasn't it? Everybody always wanted

something different. Her husband David had wanted power. He had wanted to be in charge; he had wanted to be admired. Not physically, but for his managerial abilities, for his strength and command. Sylvia just wanted to be admired, just wanted to be hungered for. Her sex drive had never dropped off. David's didn't seem to be pointed towards her anymore.

Sylvia stepped out, and then suddenly threw herself back around the corner. There was a group of women walking along. Sylvia rolled her towel up over her blonde hair, rubbing it down as if it was wet as the women passed. She wasn't sure how that was going to work. She wasn't near a shower, but at least her face was covered. The women didn't stop chatting about where they were going to eat dinner that night. So far, so good.

That was another thing. Sylvia had to sit every evening while David was blabbering on, entertaining the round table. The man she had come for, the man she had sought, wasn't there. The evenings were spent without him. Then there were the occasional glimpses, occasional moments, and finally it had turned into full-on enjoyment.

Except somebody had walked in. Her lover's face had seemed angry, truly annoyed. He'd been late arriving. That had annoyed her, too. She'd been on that walking machine for over half an hour longer than she should have before disappearing into the other room. Her lover had told her that was fine. She'd worked up a sweat. He said she always looked better when she sweated. That had done it for Sylvia. She was always one who liked to be talked about, especially about her looks, about her body, about the way she reacted to stimuli.

She rolled the towel back down, tried to fix her hair as best she could, and stepped back out into the corridor. It had been good, after all. Until they'd been interrupted, it had been wonderful. She remembered her first time back in the day, and she thought this was probably better. She wished David could have seen her. Not from some kinky idea, but just so he could understand what he was missing out on. Even at her age, she was something else.

Even at my age. Why do I talk like that? Why do I turn round and see age as something wrong? I'm still the exciting woman I was before. After all, I can still bag the younger man.

She smiled, then twisted her head as someone walked around the corner. She didn't say hello, merely passed him by, keeping her face turned, wondering if she looked awkward.

As she got closer to the cabin, she realised there were people from the other cabins around hers. She was in the better quarters, the cabins near the top. You didn't get as many people here, but you tended to know each other. She certainly didn't want to meet any of them, because David no doubt would have spoken to husbands. He'd investigate any strange sightings about his wife.

She needed that shower. She needed to be cleaned up, get into something else that didn't say she'd been at the gym. Maybe the sighting of the gym would get out. She wondered if the woman who had barged in would tell someone else. Then the rumour would spread, so they would need to have been somewhere else. It was what she feared, David finding out, and divorcing her.

She was quite happy with his money, now she had got used to the idea of him not putting her as his number one. She would happily be entertained by younger men. Those other women could keep their painting, their bowling club, their walks, their idle chat in coffee shops. Sylvia was here to live, nothing more and nothing less.

She unzipped the side pocket of her jacket, taking out her access card for the cabin. It was more than a cabin, though; it was a stateroom, which at least gave her a bit of room if David and she were both in it. He had one of those studies and he kept disappearing off to it, while often she would lie out on the balcony. That was when she didn't have any activities planned, didn't have someone to meet.

She stole quickly forward towards her cabin door. Someone came along the corridor and she froze before looking into the face of a Mexican man. He was wearing a white jacket. It was one of the staff. 'Good day,' he said, passing by. She nodded back to him, but her face was half turned away. Nobody would listen to him, anyway. Why did she care about him?

Sylvia raced to her door, put the key card up, and pushed the door open. She opened it quickly and stepped inside. Looking into the stateroom in front of her, she closed the door behind her. Sylvia realised her husband was sitting on the end of the large sofa. She watched closely, not stepping further inside the room. He was motionless, truly motionless. Maybe he was in a deep sleep. This was a good thing, a wonderful thing.

Quietly, she stepped past the sofa, staying as far away from it as possible. Slowly, she climbed up the set of stairs, and the bedroom and the study. Entering the bedroom, she quickly took off her clothes, hanging them up before jumping into the shower.

Sylvia breathed a sigh of relief as she washed herself, cleaning away her indiscretions. He hadn't seen her. He didn't know what she was up to. Now she was in the shower, she would come down and maybe sit outside. That's what she would do. She would get a drink and she would sit outside looking at the scenery. She would need to dress in something casual, simple, certainly not sporty. Take away all connections with the gym.

Her name would be there though, wouldn't it? She'd have to say she'd been to the gym. They hadn't seen her leave, had they? They didn't book people in and out, they just booked that you were there. That would be okay.

Sylvia stepped out of the shower, took one of the large towels and dried herself. Stepping into the bedroom, she listened. There was no sound from down below. He really was asleep. Had he been up late last night? She didn't know; she'd gone to bed and couldn't remember when he came in.

She found herself new underwear and then stepped into a snug pair of jeans with a blouse on top. She took a body warmer, zipping it up and put on some boots. Outside wouldn't be that warm, but she'd need to go out there and sit in the chair as if she'd been there for a while.

Sitting down after dressing and looking into the vanity mirror, Sylvia brushed her hair. She looked at the chain around her neck dangling in her cleavage. Again, she touched it. It had been the only thing she'd had on, the only thing when she'd had her moment. She remembered the dangling of the chain, its motion, and she beamed. It was quite something, wasn't it? She had looked fantastic.

Sylvia continued to brush her hair until she was sure it was right and then stood up from the front of the vanity mirror. Slowly, she walked out of the bedroom and onto the stairs that led down to the stateroom below. He was still there on the sofa, still motionless. Sylvia slowly made her way down and over to the drinks' cabinet, taking out a tumbler along with a bottle of whisky. She poured herself a generous, neat measure, her heart still pounding even though she was back.

'Are you going to sleep there the whole time? I'm going to go out onto the balcony.'

There was no response. She turned and walked out to the balcony, putting her feet up on one table as she sat on the chair, slowly sipping her whisky. The views were good, but it wasn't what excited Sylvia. She stared out there anyway, in case David awoke. He needed to see her enjoying the scenery and not just basking in the afterglow of her previous pursuit.

She couldn't believe how he could just sit there, anyway. How could he be that tired? What had he been doing? She looked across. His face looked wrong. When people were sleeping, everything was relaxed. His cheeks didn't. She hadn't really looked at him. She had tried to stay away from him, tried to keep her distance. No, he didn't look right. He didn't look well. She walked over towards him.

'David?' she said. 'David?' concern was rising in her voice. 'David, are you okay? David, are you awake?'

She stopped about a metre away, looking at him closely. Down the front of his shirt, there was that some sort of stain? Ketchup? Something he had dropped. That wasn't the shirt he was wearing earlier on either, she thought. When she had got up earlier on, he wasn't putting that on. In fact, he rarely wore that shirt. Come to think of it, he wasn't really dressed as David would dress.

Something went off in the back of her mind. A reaction to the image before her made her wonder. She reached forward, putting her hand on his shoulder, and gave him a gentle shake. As she did so, his head toppled forward, hit his thighs before tumbling onto the floor, and rolled over, completing several rotations before coming to a stop.

Sylvia said nothing at first. Her eyes were wide, her hand

still on the man's shoulder. She looked from his head to his body and then she screamed.

Sylvia ran forward, racing for the door, almost tripping over. She pulled open the door as quickly as she could. Outside in the corridor, several people stopped to look at her.

'He's dead,' she screamed. 'He's dead.' A man rushed forward. 'Who's dead?'

'My husband. His, his, his . . .'

She wanted to say head, but the words wouldn't come out and she pointed towards their cabin door. The man raced to it, tried to open it, but the door had shut.

'Have you got your key card? Have you got the access card?'

It was inside. She had left it inside. It wasn't on her. She crumbled down to her knees.

'You don't want to see,' she yelled. 'I don't want to see.'

She collapsed on the floor, closing her eyes, but failing to stop the sight of her dead husband from being the one thing she had to look at.

Chapter 10

Macleod approached the Durston cabin along with Jane and saw the ship's doctor standing outside the door. He was holding an entry card and held up his hand as Macleod approached.

'I'm thinking that your good lady probably wants to remain outside.'

'She's with me,' said Macleod. Then he stopped, catching the look on the man's face.

'I appreciate that, sir, but it's not pretty. It's really not pretty.'

Macleod turned to Jane, who had screwed her face up slightly. 'I'm going to need to take photographs, so why don't you talk to the widow,' he said. 'See if you can discover anything, or at least give her a comforting arm.'

'Okay,' said Jane.

'I'll be doing photographs,' said Macleod, 'and I'll see if you need to look at them.' Jane felt like a shiver went through her. Macleod watched her shudder and he was thankful that the doctor had spoken up.

'Just be careful too,' said Jane.

'It's all right,' said Macleod. 'I've seen plenty of bodies and I've seen them in not very nice states. You never get used to it,

but you learn how to deal with it. It can be quite a shock. I've
seen Clarissa struggle.'

Jane raised her eyebrows and then took herself off down the
corridor before stopping.

'Doctor, where is the widow?' asked Jane.

'She's down in the medical centre.' The doctor waved at one
of the crew. 'Can you escort Jane down to the medical centre?'
he said. 'Show her to Mrs Durston, Sylvia Durston,' he said, in
case Jane didn't know.

'Be there soon,' said Macleod, 'as soon as I get photographs
done.' Macleod looked for the photographer who was there
last time. The first officer was still standing outside the door,
the camera now hanging from his hand.

'Are you all right?' asked Macleod.

'I don't think anyone should go in except yourself and myself.
I'll clear up afterwards,' said the doctor. 'Put everything in the
necessary bags and storage, but in the meantime, I don't want
anybody else in here who doesn't have to be.'

'Okay,' said Macleod. He walked over to the first officer
with the camera, took it off him. 'I take it the camera's
straightforward,' he said.

'I've got it on automatic, sir,' said the first officer. 'Turn the
section at the front, it'll zoom you closer, opposite for further
away. Tap the button and then press it fully. When you tap it,
it'll go into focus. If you have problems, I'll try to come in.'

'No,' said Macleod. 'It'll be fine. I'm sure the doctor can help
me if I struggle with the technology.'

He turned and followed the doctor in through the door.
The doctor stopped, waiting for the door to close behind him
before he moved fully inside the cabin. Macleod stood in the
doorway for a moment. He could see the headless body sitting

on the sofa. His eyes cast down to the floor to see where the rest of the man was.

'Pretty brutal,' said the doctor.

'Indeed, and amazingly clean.'

'He wasn't killed here. He wasn't killed on that sofa,' said the doctor. Macleod simply nodded. It was obvious even to Macleod that it wasn't the case.

'What do you think, then?' asked Macleod.

'I've had a look around and, well, I'm suggesting the shower upstairs. The thing is that Mrs Durston has had a shower in there since, so we could go through the waste water of the vessel. We would find his blood, probably, and that would confirm it came from somewhere, but it wouldn't confirm that shower. I don't know if it's been scrubbed before Mrs Durston got in. I've neglected to inform her of that information.'

'Keep her ignorant of that,' said Macleod. 'Doctor, given the injury, there's no way you could drag a body in here like that. You'd have to have bagged it. You'd get blood everywhere, wouldn't you?'

'You can see from his shirt,' said the doctor, 'there's still blood seeped out and through. I would suggest they did it elsewhere, possibly, and I would suspect in the shower within this cabin. Washed it all away and then brought him down.'

'They changed his shirt and clothing.'

'So it would seem,' said the doctor. 'There's no way you could have done that sort of injury to a person and not have covered them in blood. The shower would be a good place. You could contain most of it and you could wash it away. You could clean the shower down.'

'It would take you time,' said Macleod, 'Wouldn't it?'

'Indeed, it would. But not that long, I don't think. One of the key things, though, would be to change the clothing quickly. He's dead, and rigor mortis is going to set in. You've got to be reasonably quick. Not within a couple of minutes, but it's going to come to a point where he'd end up breaking his arms trying to put a shirt on.'

'If the clothing is his, it's come from here. Everything says he was killed in the cabin at the moment. Certainly, pointing that way.'

'I'm sure your forensic people could have confirmed it for you, but I don't have that level of expertise,' said the doctor.

'I'll need to look and see if anyone's been accessing the cabin,' said Macleod. He took photographs, coming in from different angles, treading carefully around the room. He then went upstairs and photographed the bathroom, the bedroom, the study, and the small stairs that led up to him. Following that, Macleod went outside, photographed the balcony, both up and down, off the edge as well.

'I think I've seen enough, doctor,' said Macleod. 'Do you want any help with the body to get it into a bag? I don't think you should bring anyone else in to do this.'

'Thank you,' said the doctor. 'I'll be back in a moment.'

The doctor left the room, leaving Macleod with the body. His mind began to think about the first victim. Was there any connection between Kilmartin and Durston? They were both in the better cabins. That was certainly true. Both had wives. He knew nothing about Durston at this point. Then there was, of course, the professor. Did he know either of them? Did his daughter?

They were a slightly different couple. Would the professor have a reason for killing him? The mode of despatch was varied too, one was strangled, the next one decapitated. Was there a reason for that? It appeared as if the head had fallen off the body.

Initial reports to Macleod had said that Sylvia Durston had disturbed it. It was a very sick joke, one that Macleod was not appreciative of. The doctor returned with a black body bag. He produced a pair of gloves for Macleod.

'Here you go, Inspector. It's not the worst I've ever had to deal with. As you said, it looks like he was cleaned up elsewhere.'

'It's far from the worst I've seen as well,' said Macleod. 'Let's hope it's the last one on this cruise.'

'You think it won't be?'

'If you were the press, Doctor, I would say no comment. As you're not, and you're assisting me, I expect you to keep whatever I say now under your hat. We've had two people killed in expensive cabins. Both, while their better half has been out. There's some sort of pattern here. I can't establish what. The trouble with patterns is that they seem to keep going on and on, so yes, I'm fearing we may have a serial killer on our hands.'

Scene break, scene break, scene break.

Jane entered the medical suite behind the crew member who had taken her there. She looked over at a nurse and asked for Sylvia Durston.

'She's in the room over there. Who might you be?'

'I'm working with Detective Chief Inspector Macleod. My name's Jane Hislop.'

'Very good,' said the nurse. 'I warn you, she's in quite a state.'

Jane was shown into a room where, lying on a medical bed,

was Sylvia Durston. Tears were still streaming down her eyes. Jane approached slowly.

'My name's Jane Hislop. You can call me Jane. I'm working with Detective Chief Inspector Macleod. He's asked me to come and see you. Make sure you're okay and—'

'Okay?' said Sylvia suddenly. 'How the hell could I be okay?'

'Of course you're not. I meant to make sure that you were medically okay.'

'Right,' said Sylvia.

'Must have been a shock coming back to that scene.'

'I walked past him,' said Sylvia. 'I actually walked past him.'

'How?' asked Jane.

'I was at the gym. I was coming back from the gym and entered the cabin. He was sitting asleep, or so I thought, on the far end of the sofa. I crept past him, climbed the stairs to the bedroom. Took a shower. Got dressed. Fixed my hair. Came all the way back down. Took a drink. Sat outside. It's only when I came back in after that, I noticed—I noticed the—it was the . . .'

The woman was struggling to expand on what was happening. She turned away from Jane, looking at the wall.

'You saw something on him. It obviously showed that all was not well,' said Jane. The woman turned suddenly, her face almost white. 'I tapped his shoulder, and his head fell off.'

Jane nearly blurted out, nearly asked the question, how? She didn't want to know and knew that the scene wasn't particularly good. Instead, she thought she should focus on something else.

'Did you see anybody when you left?'

'No, I'd left some time before.'

'Was he on the sofa at that point?'

'No, he was working, I believe. I went to the gym.'

'Do you work out a lot?'

'Not overly, but it's a great gym here. There's plenty to do in it,' said Sylvia.

The answer seemed a little stale. 'What type of exercises do you tend to go for?' asked Jane.

'I—well, weights really.'

She didn't look like a woman that did weights, as little as Jane knew about them.

'What sort? The machines or the dumb weights?'

'The dumb weights,' she said. 'I stand and lift them.'

'What sort of weight do you lift? Sorry, just interested. I do some myself,' Jane lied.

'Right. Probably about thirty kilos.'

'On a single side?'

'Yes,' said Sylvia.

That sounded awfully heavy to Jane. Especially on a single side.

'What brought you back from the gym?' asked Jane.

The woman seemed to react at that point. Seemed to jar. Then she said, 'I just finished my workout. It was time to come back and get a shower. Meet up with David. I guess I'll not be meeting up with him again.'

Sylvia turned and looked at the wall. Jane wondered if she could gain any more from her. Instead, she took a trip down to the gym. Arriving there, she asked the receptionist if she could take a tour of the weights. The receptionist looked Jane up and down.

'Oh, no, I'm not intending to lift any. I just need to have a look at them.'

The receptionist seemed a bit bemused. She took Jane

through to a young man dressed in the ship's logo. He had a pair of shorts and a t-shirt on, and was in extremely good shape.

'Can I ask something?' said Jane. 'Would you expect me to lift a thirty-kilogram weight in one hand?'

The man laughed. 'You don't do those. Nobody really would do something like that. You're getting more into proper heavy lifting.'

'Very good,' said Jane. 'What sort of weight would I lift?'

'A kilo or two, maybe. Maybe up to five. Certainly, on a hand weight, you wouldn't go much above that.'

'Did you have any excitement here today?'

'Well, there was a rumour that certain people were getting up to no good in a nearby storeroom.'

'What do you mean by no good?' asked Jane.

'Get together,' said the man, slightly embarrassed.

Jane thought, *he must think I'm like his mum asking him this. No wonder he's getting red-cheeked.*

'Would you have the names of everyone that booked into the gym at that time?'

'Yes,' said the man, 'absolutely,' and turned to walk off to the receptionist. Jane looked around the gym and saw several different people. There were the types who were just there recreationally, some working out extensively. Others trying it for the first time, by the looks of it. Maybe just there because they were on holiday.

Sylvia Durston looked well, Jane thought. She looked like a trim woman, certainly kept her figure, but she was no power lifter. Sylvia had snuck in past her husband, gone and had a shower immediately afterwards.

Jane stopped for a moment and thought. She wondered if

she was putting two and two together and getting one hundred and fifty. She wondered if it was just her mind being a little too active.

Occasionally, Seoras would describe her as frisky, because he certainly wasn't like that. She smiled. She had said that Alessandra had been very like Sandy Kilmartin. Jane wasn't quite as convinced of Sylvia Durston, not from seeing her, but then the woman had suffered a major shock. The other evidence around her said it was certainly a possibility that her eyes roved as well.

The man came back with a list from the reception of all those who'd been here. Jane thanked him and then strode out of the gym area, marching back up the corridors. She almost clapped her hands, so excited that she may even give Seoras some actual evidence.

Chapter 11

Macleod wore a shirt and tie as he approached the dining room. He had popped back to the cabin to freshen up and said he would meet Jane for dinner that evening. They'd been given a special table, small and quiet, discreetly tucked away in one of the most upmarket dining rooms. As he arrived at the table, she stood up wearing a rather elegant-looking dress.

'I didn't think we were going formal,' said Macleod.

'I haven't really worn it any other time, have I? At best, we'll get an hour and a half together to sit down and eat. Maybe we could try to forget about the case for a bit.' Macleod raised his eyebrows and Jane laughed. 'I'm only kidding, Seoras. How could you stop thinking about a case when it's on? I know I have to wait until it's all done.'

Macleod gave a nod, stepped forward and kissed her on the cheek.

'Again, I'm sorry. I didn't want to take this on.' She looked at him, narrowing her eyes. 'Okay, yes, of course, I wanted to take it on once I knew it was afoot, but I didn't want there to be a murder on our holiday, never mind two murders.'

'Did you call through to the team, advise them of the other

victim?'

'I did,' said Macleod. 'I should hear from Ross sometime this evening. I just wish there was something to go on. The trouble at the moment is I've got these two victims and a Professor Flores, and there's nothing to link them, well, at least on the boat. They have a big cabin. That's it. That's all we've got.'

'Do we know why they booked?'

'We're only getting the view from the women. It looks like a routine holiday.'

'Of course, if they're covering up, they would say that, wouldn't they?'

'That's always the problem, Jane. Whatever you hear from people, take it with a pinch of salt. You must try to work out the other angles and what people are about. It's an art form. It takes practice. I haven't been a police officer for this long for no reason. I'm well trained.'

'Seoras, I found something out,' said Jane suddenly, too excited to keep in her news. 'Sylvia Durston went to the gym beforehand. When I went down there today, apparently there was an incident in one of the storerooms.'

'What sort of incident?' asked Macleod. He picked up the bottle of water on the table and poured some for Jane and some for himself.

'Well, that's the thing. Somebody was caught at it in the storeroom.'

'Sorry?' said Macleod. 'At what?'

'At it, Seoras. You know that thing you and I do occasionally, except we don't do it in a storeroom?'

Macleod almost blushed, but he recovered himself, nodding. 'And who was caught?' he said.

'That's the thing. They've disappeared. Sylvia Durston was

down at the gym. We know that. Her name's on the list. She admitted to that, but she said she'd done her workout. When I asked her about how she worked out, she talked about weights, but then she talked about lifting a weight that nobody in their right mind would lift. It just showed a complete lack of knowledge about what she claimed to do. She doesn't look like a woman who lifts weights. She's in good shape, but that might come more from aerobic exercise. I confirmed with the young man on duty. He said they didn't have weights in the size that she said. I thought I'd best get a list of all the people who were signed into the gym around that time, to see if she was with any of them.'

'Whoa,' said Macleod, 'you're saying that she's now the woman in the storeroom?'

'Well, I'm not saying it, am I? What I'm saying, Seoras, is that her story makes little sense. So clearly, she wasn't doing what she said she was doing in the gym. If you were, you'd just say.'

'So do you think she was off in a storeroom with a man?' asked Macleod.

'It makes sense, doesn't it, Seoras? It makes sense. I'm not just talking off my head.'

'This is a possibility,' said Macleod. 'We always must keep in mind it could be something else, but it's certainly interesting. I'm going to get these names on this list and get them to Ross, but they're all on board. So, what I'll do after we have our dinner is we'll go looking.'

'I'll come with you,' said Jane.

'No,' said Macleod. 'We'll need to know where they are, and it's best if it's handled by one of the crew. I'll go round with them. We don't want to look like an entourage piling around. Better keep it quieter. Besides, you could do with a rest. It gets to you.'

'What gets to you?' asked Jane.

'Detecting, the case, constantly thinking for long periods of time. Focusing on what's going on.'

'You don't come home for the first forty-eight hours. You're actually taking it quite easy at the moment.'

'I'm not,' said Macleod, 'but I can see it in you. You are tired.'

'You are right there, but I don't want to spend tonight in that bed alone. I want you in with me by midnight.'

'Okay,' said Macleod. 'I'll do my best.'

'You will do your best. There might be somebody waiting for you when you get in. I'm not promising it's going to be like a storeroom effort, but . . .'

Macleod's eyebrows raised. 'I don't think that's the appropriate language for dinner, is it?'

He was teasing her. He knew fine, she just wanted a bit of time with him. Macleod was worried for her, being on a case, thinking through things, turning them over in your mind. It took a toll, a toll he was well used to and one he could handle. Ideally, Jane wouldn't be doing this with him, but he had no one else to trust. And she'd just come up with a cracking lead.

They sat through a three-course dinner together, idly chatting about other things at home. Jane was mentioning the garden and what she planned to do, and the possibility of taking up some other sports. Macleod was impressed with the activities she did. She mentioned about Clarissa getting back to golf as well. She'd asked Jane to join her. Quite what they would talk about when on the golf course, Macleod didn't know, but he found it slightly disconcerting.

With the dinner complete, Macleod saw Jane to their cabin, telling her to have a shower. He, meanwhile, made his way up to the bridge, reported to the Captain what he was doing, and asked for some help to go round the list Jane had procured. Melanie was ordered to take Macleod round the vessel.

She was a cheerful soul, and Macleod was quite happy to have her along. If somebody got edgy about the fact that they'd been disturbed, Melanie's face would certainly be more comforting than Macleod's. It was like Hope, or even Cunningham, Ross even. In fact, anyone except Clarissa or him. The others seemed to have a calming effect on people. With Macleod, people just seemed to get worried he was on to them, and with Clarissa, panic set in because nobody was sure what was going to happen.

For the next two hours, Macleod wandered round with Melanie, ringing doors and confirming the people who were there. Most were couples or at least friends and were unaware of the storeroom incident. However, Macleod found a woman who admitted to being the person who had seen the illicit activity. She had told her friend, and the rumour had started up from there.

'Would you be able to identify them again?' asked Macleod.

'No,' said the woman. 'I turned away almost instantly. I mean, you don't expect that sort of thing, do you?'

'What were you going into the storeroom for?' he asked.

'I wasn't. Got the wrong door.'

Macleod's face fell after the conversation, and Melanie asked him what was up.

'Oh, it's a witness, a witness who cannot identify anyone. She's possibly the most useless witness going. It's like having a helmsman who doesn't know how to steer a ship or plot a course.'

'There's still time, though. We haven't seen everybody on

the list.'

Melanie smiled at him and Macleod picked up. It was like having a daughter there, ready to pick you up, ready to boost you. Although having talked to friends who had children, he wasn't so sure that's what most of them did.

Macleod and Melanie made their way to an interior cabin, looking for the last person on the list they hadn't come across yet. It was a Jürgen Heinz, and they'd already rang the doorbell but had got no answer from the cabin. Once again, they rang it to no avail and so rang the cabin next door. An older woman stepped out.

'Hello?' she said. 'Can I help?' Melanie beamed. Macleod stepped forward.

'I'm Detective Chief Inspector Macleod. I'm looking to speak to Jürgen Heinz, who's your next-door neighbour. Have you seen him on this trip?'

'Once or twice. Not recently, though.'

'What does he look like?'

'You don't know?' said the woman. 'You're looking for a man and you don't know what he looks like?'

'I'm making very basic enquiries.'

'Into what?' asked the woman.

'A little indiscretion,' said Macleod. So far, the rumours of murder on the ship had not exploded. Amongst the crew there may have been talk, but the passengers were not being spoken to, and Macleod had the Captain to thank for that. He'd issued an embargo to the crew about discussing the killings outside of crew quarters. He would discipline anyone who mentioned what had happened. Outside of that, those affected have been down in the medical centre, and were advised not to speak about it to anyone outside of those investigating.

'I haven't seen him recently. He was in the cabin on his own. I believe he's, whoa, about his late thirties, maybe not quite into his forties. And he's, uh, he's a sprightly-looking man. Blond hair.'

Macleod noted down the details in a small notebook. 'And the last day you saw him?' he asked.

'That would have been over five days ago.'

'Have you not been worried having not seen him about?'

'I'm on holiday, Inspector. I'm not here to check up on my neighbours. He could have met up with some woman and been living in her cabin for all I know. He said hello to me. That was it. We haven't really discussed or spoken about anything.'

Macleod nodded and thanked the woman, and then suggested that he and Melanie go to the bridge. Walking back, Melanie asked Macleod what he was up to.

'Well, I need the Captain's permission to go into that cabin. I will not break into it. It's someone who may still be on the ship and just haven't accessed it lately. The neighbour could be right. Well, I will not barge in and upset the man. I have no definite evidence that he's actually involved with the case. We're just running through enquiries. If I thought he was involved, I would have told you to open up the door, but this is the Captain's vessel, and I'll make sure I run things past him.'

'Very good, sir,' said Melanie and took Macleod to the Captain. He was in his ready room.

'Do you have any suspicions about him?' asked the Captain.

'No, I just wish to see and eliminate him from our enquiries.'

'Very good. Melanie, take Macleod down, and you can open the door.'

'Just before we go, can I see the last time it was accessed?'

The Captain took Macleod off to the room full of computers.

The Captain logged in and made some connections. He turned round and said, 'it hasn't been accessed in days. Maybe four.'

'Interesting,' said Macleod. 'Let's go, Melanie. Quick.'

Although they didn't run all the way to the cabin, they certainly made with despatch. As they arrived, Melanie produced her access card, tapping it on the panel outside the door. It changed from red to green and she pushed open the door, but Macleod held her back. He said, 'I'll go first.'

Melanie looked at him in surprise. Clearly, she thought he was far older than her and therefore she should protect him, but Macleod pushed on through. The cabin had twin beds, one on either side. There was a washroom and a little shower area, but it was tiny, even smaller than Macleod's original cabin. But what Macleod did notice was, there was absolutely no evidence anyone had been in here.

'These beds haven't been slept in,' said Melanie.

'No,' said Macleod. 'I'm not sure that we'll find Jürgen Heinz.'

'Why? What does it all mean?' asked Melanie. 'You don't just hire a cabin and then not use it.'

'It depends. I think what we don't want to do is hang about here for too long. However, I would like the Captain to observe whether anyone comes in here again on the voyage. Maybe he can set up some sort of alert on the system?'

'I'm still not following,' said Melanie, as they came out and she locked the door. As they strolled down the corridors, Macleod lowered his voice.

'The thing, Melanie, is that if you're going to kill someone, and especially on a boat like this, what do you do if you think you're discovered? On land, you can run away. You can't run anywhere here. He may have several rooms, a few disguises. Jürgen Heinz may be the man we want, even if that's not his real name.'

Macleod returned to report to the Captain, asking him to set up an alarm on the door function. The Captain did so, and Macleod retired back to his cabin. It was only half-eleven. He'd made good time, and Jane would be ready for him.

Macleod approached his own door, accessed it, and on entering, found that the lights were out. He used the dimmer switch to put them on at a low level, crept up the stairs, and approached the bedroom. He opened the door gingerly, looking in.

There was light snoring going on, and he could see Jane with the duvet tucked up around her. Once inside, he turned around, switched off the lights in the sitting room and entered the bedroom before changing into his pyjamas. Moving the covers back, he slid into the bed and then put his arms around Jane. He pulled himself close and suddenly felt her wake up.

'Is that you, Seoras?' she said.

'Well, you would kind of hope so, wouldn't you?' he said. He got a slight slap on his thigh.

'I'm awake now,' she said, but he could hear the tiredness in her voice.

'And I'm here,' he said. 'Back to sleep. I told you it wears you out, this. It really does.'

'Sorry,' she said.

'Nothing to be sorry about. When we're shot of the case, there'll be plenty more days at sea.' He pulled her tight and then lay with his head lying on the back of her neck. He tried to think about Jane, but within a minute, Macleod had fallen asleep.

Chapter 12

Ross put his head down, tapping away on the keyboard, and then would flick his eyes up occasionally to the screen. Macleod had sent him three names. One had lost his tie and could not explain how it had disappeared. As he searched through the records, Ross chortled to himself, thinking about Macleod wandering around the cruise ship. He couldn't imagine the boss on one, couldn't see him chilling out.

It would, of course, have been Jane's idea. Macleod's partner was always fun to be around if nothing else. Although Ross had no physical attraction towards her, as a person he enjoyed her banter and how she could lift the room. She was, in a lot of ways, a perfect foil to Macleod, taking on the inspector's dark persona.

'You all right, Als?' said a voice from the other end of the office.

'Just knee-deep, running errands for the man who's not here.'

'What?' spat Clarissa. 'What do you mean you're running errands for the man who's not here? He's off on a cruise, and she'll kill him if he's working.'

'She's working with him,' said Ross. He stood up, waving

Clarissa over.

Clarissa Urquhart, formerly of the murder team, was now working in the arts division, but she was based in Inverness Station. As such, she hadn't completely disappeared from the daily life of the team. She was there in the canteen. They would pass her in the station, and every now and again she'd pop down to say hi. She'd also heard that Ross was working towards his sergeant's exams and felt the need to come down and offer advice. The fact he had a detective inspector already there who could help him didn't seem to put Clarissa off, but then again, Clarissa never really got put off in life.

'What do you mean, *working*? How's that happening?'

'Murder on board. It's a British vessel, there's a murder on board, and he's the only policeman there. So, he's got Jane working with him, but he's been sending over stuff to us, asking for forensics to liaise with the doctors.'

'He's what? Why don't they just put it into port and get somebody to sort it? She will not be happy at that.'

'I wouldn't know about that,' said Ross. 'I haven't spoken to her. I've only spoken to the boss.'

A door opened at the side of the room, and Hope emerged from her office. 'Clarissa,' said Hope. 'Good to see you. Here for a reason?'

'Just dropping in to say hello to Als. I see he's at the grindstone. Seoras goes half the world away and you still can't get rid of him.'

'Tell me about it,' said Hope. 'At least it's been quiet here. There's nothing come up on the murder team.'

'While you're here,' said Ross, 'come look at this.'

Hope strolled down the office and stood behind Ross's chair. Clarissa, not to be outdone, joined her. Clarissa had her tartan trews on, a shawl wrapped around her, and it was clear to Ross that she was heading home, probably back to Frank. The thing about Clarissa was she was a detective. While she turned round and said that Macleod should do his own spade work, Ross could tell she was already interested in the case, despite knowing no details whatsoever.

'Warren Kilmartin,' said Ross. 'David Durston.' He turned to Clarissa. 'That's the two victims so far. Durston was decapitated, and Kilmartin was strangled and then hung up by a necktie.'

'It's not really the sort of cruise you want to be on, is it?' said Clarissa.

'But there's also this Professor Carlos Flores. Now, Flores is alive, but it was his tie that was used to hang up Kilmartin. The thing is that these people were down in Oxford together. I've traced back their histories. It's taken me the best part of a day, but they were all in Oxford, based around the University. As far as I can make out, they were members, according to the alumni document which is some thirty years old, of a Dead Rubber Society.'

'Dead Rubber Society. What on earth is a Dead Rubber Society?'

'I don't know,' said Ross, 'It doesn't say, but I know it's now defunct because it's not running anymore. Maybe it stopped several years ago. However, it says that it was run by a Filton Pritchard and John Surly.'

'Filton Pritchard,' said Clarissa. 'I know that name. Why do I know that name?' She stood looking up at the ceiling, but nothing was coming to her.

'He's in the art world. He's an art dealer.'

'Used to work on the west coast,' said Clarissa. 'If I remember rightly, fairly reputable. Can't remember anything too dodgy from him. Retired, though,' said Clarissa.

Ross nodded. 'He is, and he now lives in—'

'Tobermory. He lives in Tobermory,' said Clarissa.

'You said there was someone else there.'

'John Surly,' said Ross, 'Now, he's still living in Oxford.'

'So, what you're saying to me,' said Hope, 'is you've detailed a link between them. Flores, Kilmartin and Durston, they're all in the same group. It's been run by Filton Pritchard and John Surly. Did you check the vessel records to see if they were on board?'

'Of course I did,' said Ross. 'First thing I did, but they're not there.'

'It seems to me that you need to detail this case out to Clarissa, and do it fairly sharpish.'

'Why?' asked Ross.

'Well, as far as I can see, the only link to the murders the boss has got is Surly and Filton Pritchard. If we can find them, and find out what they really know, we may get the boss closer. Is Frank expecting you home tonight, Clarissa?' asked Hope.

'Why,' asked Clarissa, very aware that Hope never asked about her dinner plans, or indeed her home life.

'Well, as far as I can see, the boss is going to need this followed up on. With someone in the art world, it's maybe best they see a friendly face.'

Ross burst out laughing, and Clarissa hit him on the shoulder.

'I am a friendly face to some,' said Clarissa to Ross.

'You'll also be able to find out more about his life and probably get in closer. Go down to Filton and see what he knows about the Oxford Society, and those three men. Find out if there was anybody else in it, anyone else the boss would need to be worried about.'

Clarissa's face screwed up somewhat. 'I've been promising Frank I'd be coming home at a sensible time, especially with Macleod away. Frank said that there was no way he could keep me there if he's not there.'

'I need you on this one,' said Hope.

'I could go,' said Ross.

'You could, except you're going to Surly. Get down to Oxford, find him, find out what he knows.'

'Why don't you go, or Cunningham?' asked Clarissa.

'I know technically I'm not your superior. You don't work for me anymore. But in case a murder investigation comes up, I need to be here. Especially with Seoras away. I'll also have Cunningham. You two are used to working on your own. I don't want to send Cunningham all the way down there, unaccompanied.'

'Okay,' said Ross, 'I'll get on to it.'

'Do you want a lift?' said Clarissa. Ross shook his head vehemently.

'Give me a moment. I'll need to sort something out before we head off tonight.'

'Thank you,' said Hope. 'I'm sure Seoras will appreciate it, even if he doesn't say it.'

'He always says it," said Clarissa. 'Says it in his own way. Never happy. Never cheerful, but you can tell him from me that this will not happen regularly. I work in the art world. I'm only doing this because I'm not going to look at a dead body.' She turned and strode off before suddenly stopping before leaving the office.

'I am going to *not* look at a dead body? I take it that there's no likelihood this guy is going to be dead.'

'Not as far as I'm aware,' said Ross.

Hope nodded at the pair of them and walked back into her office. Ross logged off his computer. He made a quick phone call to Angus back at the house, telling him he was going to have to disappear through the night. Once he'd done that, Ross approached Hope's office, knocking on the door, and entering. He stood looking at her, or rather, looking over her shoulder at the wall. On it was a large picture of a cruise liner.

'Is that the one he's on?'

'Yes,' she said, 'There's the cabins up there. Looks like they're going for all the posh people. However, the cabin that Seoras said the missing guy was in is down below. Looks to me like this could be a serial effort. He may be after several people so you're going to need to move quick.'

'I've phoned Angus and I'm on the move tonight. I'll get there in the morning and interview Surly.'

'Thank you, Alan,' she said. She stood looking at the boat and he came up to join her.

'It's weird him being away, isn't it?' said Ross. 'He hasn't exactly called through for many conferences. It's more like he's trying to solve it on his own.'

'Apparently, he's got Jane with him. She's doing some detecting as well. Makes me wonder what I put all that effort in for.'

Ross laughed. He went to turn away and then he turned back. 'How many big cabins are there up there?'

'Twelve,' said Hope.

'Twelve potentials then. Twelve people who could die.'

'No,' said Hope. 'One of them's been taken over by Macleod. Apparently, it wasn't occupied. The Captain's so impressed with his efforts that he's actually given him one. Suppose it sweetens it for Jane, doesn't it? The Captain claimed it had a study area that meant Macleod could work undisturbed. I think the man probably realised that Jane was going to be pissed off. Offered her a little extra.'

'So, he gets an upgraded cabin, and what do I get? I take it I'm not actually sleeping tonight. I'm just driving down.'

'Yes. Drive down quick. I could hear it in his voice when he spoke to me. He's suspecting more killings. Seoras must be worried and he can't be trusting anyone because he's got Jane working with him. He wouldn't put Jane in the line of fire unless he needed her. Apparently, it was her who dug up the list from the gym that led Macleod to find that Jürgen Heinz wasn't on board or at least hadn't been to his cabin for five days. I was going to do a whiteboard. Maybe have a discussion amongst us, but you're away, so maybe I'll just do it with Cunningham.'

'Do you not trust Cunningham enough to send her this far?'

'You'll be down there on your own, and we've got dead people. Cunningham's good, and, well, ideally, I'd actually like to send her with you. But I haven't got enough people here if a case comes in. You can handle yourself, Ross. You always have.'

'Thank you. I'll get going. I'll give you a call tomorrow morning when I find the man.'

'You do that. Drive safe. It's a long trip.'

As Ross turned to walk out of the office, the door opened, and in marched Clarissa. 'Frank is not happy with you,' she said, pointing a finger at Hope.

'You can sort your own love life out,' said Hope, and then she put on her serious face to Clarissa. 'I've just told Alan, be careful. I've got two dead on that boat. Two dead, we don't know where from or why. One of them was decapitated. You may know your Filton Pritchard, but make sure you do. And if he's not about, make sure we get a photograph, some way of ID-ing him. Get descriptions just in case they're on that vessel.'

'Of course, I will do.'

Clarissa looked up at the large-scale drawing of the vessel. 'They're all posh cabins that you've circled up there, aren't they? Except for that one further down.'

'The one further back is where Jürgen Heinz is missing from. The other ones are where the victims were, and indeed our suspect.'

'Posh people's murders, then. Posh people's murders on a cruise ship. Quite classy, really, isn't it? No wonder he hasn't taken me along.'

Ross laughed. 'He's not the most comfortable around rich people, our Seoras,' said Clarissa. 'I hope Jane can help him out a bit with that. Give him a touch of class.'

'You can tell he's not here,' said Hope. 'You'd never speak like that in front of him.'

'Of course I would, and I'd also run for cover when he swung the hand.' She threw her shawl around herself again, turned and marched over to the door. 'Time to go, Als. Time for us poor plods to make our way down the country. I bet you he's living it up, too. I bet you he's in complete glamour over there.'

'He'll probably be bored to tears. Well, at least until this murder came along,' said Ross.

'You're absolutely right,' said Clarissa. 'And we're doing the dirty work. Let's get going. Time to get dirty.'

Chapter 13

W hat's our next step?' asked Jane. She was standing at the entrance to the small study area within the suite, watching Macleod running through a pad of paper with a pen.

'Sorry?' said Macleod, looking up.

'What's the next move?' asked Jane. She noticed that Macleod's head had gone quickly back down to the paper.

'Coffee, thanks.'

'Seoras,' said Jane, stepping forward and waving her hand in front of his face. 'I'm not offering you coffee. Just asking what the next move is. I'm your partner in this. You said that. You enlisted me, so I'd like to know what's going on. I stayed here when you went out and started checking cabins. Since you came back from that, you've been buried deep, writing things out, going over that pad of paper. I don't know what you're doing. I don't know what we're doing next.'

'I'm thinking,' said Macleod. 'This is what I do. I turn it over in my head. I mosey about in the office. Sometimes I go out, or I wander down to see the team. I'm chewing it over. It's how I solve things. That and, of course, going out and checking crime scenes, talking to people.'

'When are we talking to people?' asked Jane.

'Not yet. I haven't really got anybody to talk to. I searched the cabins, and we came up with one, Jürgen Heinz. His neighbour said he was in his thirties and sprightly. He has blond hair, but he hadn't been in this cabin at all. The trouble is, trying to look out for Jürgen Heinz, there's how many thousand people here? The person who saw him didn't exactly give a full description of him. Blond hair, late thirties, sprightly. What does sprightly mean?'

'What do you intend to do?'

'I'm thinking this through. Ross will come back with stuff. He sent me through some things already. I just go over and over and check and check until something comes. Something always comes, Jane. That's the way I am. I see it.'

'You're not seeing it with me at the moment. I seem to kick about and generally make you coffee. I'm not Ross.'

'What do you mean by that?'

'Ross always makes you the coffee.'

'Ross doesn't make me my coffee anymore. My secretary makes me my coffee.'

'God help her,' said Jane. Macleod looked up, and narrowed his eyes. It was casual blasphemy, but Jane never saw it that way. More of a cry for help.

'Why don't you do something?' asked Macleod. 'I'll come find you if something comes to me. Go somewhere public, though.'

'Why?' asked Jane. 'You think we're in danger?'

'I don't know,' said Macleod. 'There's somebody who's killed two people. If they know that we're investigating, we could get attacked. It's something you always carry as a police officer, but I know the signs. I know what to look out for. You don't.

108

Go somewhere public, somewhere there's other people.'

'I'm going to go down to the gym.'

'To work out?' asked Macleod, astonished.

'No. I'll go into the sauna. Sit down and have a stretch. A bit of a soak-up, and then I'll come back after that. Even get you another coffee if you haven't managed to find the kettle.'

Macleod looked up. 'I know it's rubbish,' he said. 'I don't want to be doing this any more than you do.'

'You want to be doing this a lot more than I do,' said Jane. 'This is what you do. It's what you're good at as well.'

'I'm here with you. This is our time, for us, but I can't not help out.'

'It's not a problem—well, it is,' she said. 'It's rubbish, but it is what it is. I'm not blaming you for it, Seoras. You have to do it. It's part of your job. I get that. You want me to assist you. Someone to bounce ideas off, but yet, you're not bouncing ideas off me.'

'If Hope was stood where you are, she wouldn't be getting any ideas from me either.'

'Really? Would you not pull everybody in on a conference? Would you not throw it about again? That's what I hear.'

'No. Not at this point,' said Macleod. 'Sometimes I hold it all in. Sometimes I have to pull the picture together. Go for your sauna. Take your time with it. Stay public, though. I mean that.'

'I think you're overreacting on that one.'

'Who's the police officer?' asked Macleod.

'Yes, Detective Chief Inspector,' said Jane, giving him a mock salute.

'Really?' said Macleod. 'I mean it.'

'Okay,' said Jane. 'I get it, Seoras. I'll see you in an hour or two.'

Jane turned, walked to the bedroom where she picked up her swimming costume and a small bag to place it into. She took her hairbrush and made for the front door of the large cabin.

As she walked along the corridors, making for the sauna, Jane found herself looking this way and that, trying to spot anyone who'd been involved in the affair so far. She didn't see anyone and instead mused over what was happening.

He says he sits and chews there, goes over things. Well, I can go over things, too, thought Jane. *If a guy has a cabin and he doesn't use it, does that mean it's just him? Is there someone else that he's in a cabin with? Has he got a couple of different cabins? Are there different people or is he changing disguise?* she thought. *I might just have seen too many episodes of those crime dramas on television.*

She gave her head a shake and went to sit down at the small bar beside the gym area. She decided to have a quick drink of juice before she went in. After all, it was best not to be dehydrated in a sauna. She ordered an orange juice, sat down at one chair, and looked across to the far side of the seated area. She spotted Professor Carlos Flores, but he wasn't looking at her. The bald man with the bushy eyebrows seemed to look around for someone. She wasn't sure what he was doing. She thought she'd keep an eye on him to begin with.

Jane sipped on her orange juice and noted that the professor hadn't moved off his seat. Indeed, twenty minutes later, she was sick of watching him, because the man was doing nothing of interest, yet he still seemed to be on the lookout for someone.

Well, I'm not the police officer, so I'm not sitting around, thought

Jane. *I'm on holiday. I need to relax.*

She stood up and wandered off into the women's changing rooms. Once inside, she gave her hair a quick brush, tying it up at the back. The sauna wouldn't be good for it. She could wash it tonight in the shower in the cabin. Seoras probably wouldn't even notice, anyway, fixated as he was by this case.

She didn't get annoyed at that. It's who he was. If she didn't like the fact that he got his kicks investigating things, she was with the wrong man. She wasn't. She was sure of that.

Part of her, though, remembered back to being in the house when she got attacked. A killer had eventually come for her simply because she was Macleod's partner. He had filled the bath with acid. He was ready to throw her into it when Hope had intervened. Hope still had an acid burn on her face for her trouble. Standing up now in her swimming costume, Jane felt herself shake from reliving the memory. She grabbed a towel, put it around her neck, and stepped out of the women's changing rooms. She looked over to where Professor Flores would've been, but he wasn't there anymore.

Typical, she thought. *As soon as I get up and move, he gets up and moves. Oh, well, not to worry. Seoras doesn't seem to think he's that big a suspect.*

Jane wondered why not. The man's tie had been found around the neck of Warren Kilmartin, the wealthy owner of the large sports clothing company. Surely, that gave the impression that the man was involved. Seoras seemed to think it was some kind of setup, pointing out that experienced killers rarely grab their own clothing and use it to kill someone. And then leave it behind? She thought maybe the man was in a rush, but Seoras had said there was nothing rushed about the whole killing.

Jane stepped up to sign the register for the sauna. Getting a smile from the rather young but dashy-looking attendant, she turned and made her way over to the steamed-up door. Opening it, she caught a blast of steam.

The unit was recharging itself. It did this occasionally. Normally, the sauna was quite clear from one end to the other. Every now and again, when the temperature dropped and it needed to be lifted, there came a quick blast, steam running around the sauna.

It was a funny system. She'd seen saunas before where you dropped water on hot coals and the steam came up, but this was an electric-based system firing out jets of steam. Obviously, they couldn't just light a fire in the middle of a ship. Even in the old days, that was a bad idea except for cooking. This sauna was no exception.

She sat down at the end, nearest the door, as the far end was steaming up the most. She pulled the towel around her neck tight, leaned back into it, trying to work her neck muscles, and take away some of the soreness that was running down the back. It was good to feel the heat.

She closed her eyes, drifting off for a moment, and then opened them, looking along the wooden bench she was sitting on. Something was at the far end. As the steam cleared, she looked and saw someone lying down. For a moment, she sat up and then relaxed again. She looked around the rest of the sauna but couldn't see anyone. She reached down and adjusted her swimsuit.

There was a time when she would've been quite happy to wear a bikini, but nowadays, later in the years, she would say her body wasn't up to it. That being said, her vibrant personality often attracted other men, and she didn't enjoy being out without Seoras in situations like this.

It had happened a few times. They were always older men, well, around her age, and they always had been divorced or their wife had left them for some other reason. She'd said hello back to them. She'd spoken a couple of words, and the next thing they thought they were going to be going off on a date with her.

When she pointed out that she wasn't married, but she was Macleod's partner, they went on that she couldn't be serious. After all, she hadn't married him. She knew Seoras didn't see it like that, but sometimes she felt the doubts creep in.

Jane opened her eyes again, leaning forward. The person at the far end was still lying in the exact same position. Not close to it, but spot on. She stared at the figure for a moment. If you were asleep, if you were dozing, or if you were just simply relaxing, the chest would rise and fall. This man's chest was not moving.

Jane swung her legs off the wooden bench and walked over. As she got closer, she saw red, thick, rich in colour, staining the wooden benches. She reached forward and tapped the foot of the figure. There was nothing, no motion. Then she grabbed the other foot. Again, no motion. Jane screamed.

She was suddenly grabbed from behind, and an instinct took over. As she raised her arms up, the towel trapped between them in horror, she saw a knife swinging towards her. But the towel caught it. She looked up to see the blade hanging above her.

Jane screamed again, this time slipping down from the towel, and she ran. She threw open the door of the sauna, stepped out into the gym, and reached down for a stray weight. This was one regularly used for small-scale weightlifting and some men, and indeed some women, lifted it with one hand. Jane, however, grabbed it with two, turned, and flung it behind her. She heard it clatter off someone's knee.

'You bitch,' he shouted rather too loudly. Jane didn't look behind, still running, but she heard his voice calling out to her. 'Keep out of the way! It's not your business!'

Jane bolted straight for the desk, throwing herself at it. The young man who had served earlier was down behind it, checking through some cupboards. On hearing this thud, he stood up.

'There's a body in the sauna,' said Jane, 'and that man,' she flung an arm behind her, 'he did it.'

The young man behind the desk flinched. He clearly was struggling to compute what Jane had just said.

'I said, there's a dead body and that man—' she turned and looked. There was no one there.

'I'm sorry, miss. I don't see anyone.'

Jane turned around; the man was gone. Jane turned back to the desk, reached over, and grabbed the young man's hand. She said, 'Come with me.'

They ran over to the sauna and Jane pulled open the door and pointed at the far end. The steam had cleared somewhat and lying there with a pool of blood beside him was Professor Flores. Jane stepped forward and the young man raced towards him. The attendant went to put his hands down, but Jane said no.

It didn't look like there was any life whatsoever in Flores. Even if his body was still warm, that could have been more from the sauna heat and anything else. She pulled the young man back out of the sauna, closing the door.

'You need to stay there,' she said. 'Just stand in front of it.

I'm going to get my partner.'

'Your partner. Who's your partner?'

'Detective Chief Inspector Macleod. Don't let anyone in. Don't let anyone near it, not even the Captain.'

She turned to go, and then suddenly an image flashed through her mind. She saw the knife again. Jane saw Professor Flores's body. Her legs betrayed her, and she tumbled to the ground. She lay there shaking, a cold sweat went across her face. That knife had been so close. That swing was intended to kill her, and only the towel saved her life.

Chapter 14

Macleod was going through his pad of paper for what felt like the umpteenth time. It wasn't a waste of time; it was just he never knew when something was going to strike. If you weren't making connections and you didn't know where to go, the next best thing to do was to churn over the information. Get it through your head, because something could hook in there. Something joined with something and told you what was happening. He looked over at his coffee. The cup was only half empty, but as he picked it up to taste, it was cold.

Where was Jane, anyway? She hadn't been gone that long, had she? The time didn't seem to have passed that quickly. Macleod felt he'd been thinking about things for hours. He stood up, picked up the cup, made his way down to the small kitchenette, and tipped the cup down the sink. He took a sachet of the instant coffee, put it into the cup, and then clicked on the kettle again. Yes, it was instant coffee. Although it was a decent instant coffee, he would rather have gone out to one of the ship's cafes and got himself a proper coffee. Beggars couldn't be choosers. Maybe he should have got Jane to do that.

He didn't want her to feel like she was there to serve him, run around getting the coffees, getting the food, bringing the lunch. They were on holiday. He'd asked her to help. He wanted her to feel like an equal. Although the more he got on into the investigation, the more he realised she couldn't be an equal. She didn't have the training, and he wanted to keep her away from some of the more horrific parts of what had happened. She certainly didn't want to see the head of David Durston; even for Macleod, that was a tough scene to visit. He gave a little shudder as he waited for the kettle to boil.

The steam rose, and the button went click. Macleod poured the hot water into his coffee. As he did so, the doorbell of his cabin rang. He gave a stretch and a yawn. Leaving his coffee, he walked forward down to the door. Jane had forgotten her key card, perhaps.

He looked out of the small peephole, remembering the advice he'd given to Jane. You had to take care. Times like these, with evil people about, you didn't know. You were never sure when you could be attacked. During most cases, you weren't. During most cases, unless you were hunting someone down and were on the trail, you were perfectly safe. This killer was clearly after specific people, but if you got in the way, whoever you were, you could be at risk.

Through the peephole, Macleod saw the first officer and opened his cabin door.

'Hello there. I'm just working on something. Was the Captain looking for an update?'

'No, inspector, I'm afraid there's been an incident.'

Macleod's heart jumped. 'Jane?' he asked.

'She's fine,' said the first officer. 'Well, not fine, but she's uninjured and in the safe hands of the crew.'

Macleod was in his shirt sleeves and trousers, and he turned quickly, running inside the cabin to grab his jacket. He came back out, telling the first officer they needed to go quickly.

As they strode through the corridors, the first officer advised Jane had been attacked, but that she hadn't been injured. Macleod's pace only quickened as the man spoke.

Macleod arrived at the gym area to see Jane sitting up with the doctor attending to her. She looked a little woozy and there was a crowd around her with two of the crew protecting the entrance to the sauna.

'Jane,' said Macleod, rushing forward. He sank down to his knees and enveloped her in his arms, and she hugged him back tightly.

'Easy,' said the doctor. 'She's had a fright. I think she's still a little woozy.'

Macleod moved back slightly and looked at her face. He could see the tension all over it.

'He tried to stab me,' said Jane.

'Easy,' said Macleod. 'Just take it easy. It's all right.'

He leaned forward again, hugging her, holding her tight, whispering reassurance to her. Part of him saw a victim, someone panicked by the situation they'd been put in. They were struggling to comprehend what had happened, but there was the other part of him who just saw Jane.

Macleod wanted to find whoever had done this. He wanted to rip them apart. He wanted to be everything that an outstanding police officer wasn't.

'I've protected the crime scene,' said the first officer. 'Nobody's been in since Jane was, along with the killer. Oh, and our assistant, Antonio there. He briefly went in with her.'

Macleod turned and looked towards Antonio, a young lad

clearly in his early twenties. Antonio was a strapping lad, and he seemed to be less affected by the sight he'd witnessed than Jane was.

'Did you see what was in there as well?' asked Macleod.

'Yes, I did.'

Macleod held up his hand. 'I'll talk to you in a minute. Not out loud. She needs to refocus. She needs to calm down.'

'Yes, she does,' said the doctor. 'As you can see, she's physically okay. If you want to get on, inspector, and look at the scene, I'm happy to look after her. She'll only be here. I'm not going anywhere without informing you first.'

Macleod looked into Jane's face. She stared back at him.

'Go, Seoras, go. You need to look into this. You need to move quickly on it. I'm not okay, but I will be. The doctor will look after me. It's just a shock. I'm physically okay. He didn't lay a hand on me.'

Macleod nodded, leaned forward, and kissed her on the forehead. 'Take it slow and easy,' he said. 'Take care of her, doctor.'

Macleod stood up and walked over to Antonio. He was beside the gym reception desk, but Macleod pulled him away to the corner of the room.

'Can you explain what happened?'

'Not really,' he said. 'I was down behind the counter, sorting things out in the cupboards down there. I heard the lady come rushing out. By the time I looked up, she was telling me that someone had been in the sauna with her, but he was gone.

'You didn't see him at all?'

'No,' he said.

'What about the scene inside? Quietly,' said Macleod, 'if you would.'

'I only went in briefly. The lady took me in and there's a body at the far end. There's blood around it.

'Is it a dead body?' asked Macleod.

'Looked dead to me.'

'Has anybody checked?'

'I don't know,' said Antonio.

Macleod walked over to the doctor, tapping him on the shoulder. He stood up and moved away from Jane for a moment. Macleod whispered to him, 'Has anybody actually been inside to check if that's a dead body?'

'Not that I'm aware of. I think it's been sealed.'

'Get one of the crew to stay with Jane for a moment. I need you in with me. Quickly doctor.'

Macleod walked over to the sauna, waving the two makeshift guards to either side. He opened the door using a handkerchief from his pocket and stepped inside to the hot and claustrophobic air. He looked to the far end, spying the body of a man in swimming trunks, lying on the wooden bench. The colouration around the bench was definitely dark, possibly blood-like. The doctor entered behind him.

'You go first, doctor. Just quickly, once over, make sure he is dead. If not, let's get moving.'

The doctor brushed past Macleod and stepped up close to the body. He took a look at an incision around the neck.

'The throat's been slashed. That's where all the blood's come from,' said the doctor. 'Come closer. He's definitely dead. There's no movement anywhere. He couldn't have survived that for long.'

Macleod nodded and walked over, staring at the body. 'Thank you, doctor. If you take care of Jane and then as soon as you're happy she's okay, please come and take a further look at the body. See if you can find anything else out. Contact our forensic department.'

'I will do. As for your partner,' said the doctor, 'she'll be fine. Physically, she's fine. Mentally, I think it's just shock at the moment. I would advise that you monitor what she sees, what she dreams. Make sure that she's not trying to push back anything that's coming into her mind.'

'Thank you,' said Macleod. He understood victims from experience and the police courses, which told him all about what could happen to them. Macleod didn't get to deal with a lot of them, not in an extended sense. He was always there to see whatever it was he could pull from them, as opposed to help with their rehabilitation.

Macleod looked at the throat wound running right across the neck. He looked at the blood on the floor, keeping his feet clear. Someone had slashed a man across the throat. The man, of course, was Professor Flores. He recognised the bald head and busy eyebrows. There would have to be a formal identification from the daughter, but it was him. Macleod looked around the sauna, up and down for any clues, and stepped outside and asked the first officer for the camera.

It took ten minutes to get it, and then Macleod stepped back inside the sauna, operating the shutter from as many angles as he could. Happy he'd captured the scene, he returned outside, feeling the sweat dripping off his brow. He could not stand saunas to begin with. Why would anyone want to sit in the heat? Need their head examined.

He saw Jane getting to her feet alongside the doctor.

'I think you should head back to our cabin,' said Macleod to Jane.

'Seoras,' she said. 'I've had a thought.' She was shaking.

The doctor stepped forward. 'I agree with the inspector. You should go back to your cabin. I think we should send someone with her.'

'One of the ladies from the crew,' said Macleod. 'Maybe you should go for a lie-down, Jane, and we'll put two crew on the door, please, doctor.'

The doctor nodded, turned to the first officer, but Jane grabbed Macleod by the wrist.

'Seoras, listen, I'm trying to tell you something.' He turned and saw her shaking face.

'The killer, is he coming as different people? I was thinking this, he wasn't in the cabin. If he's not in that cabin, maybe he's got several cabins, maybe he's disguised, maybe he's being different people to different victims. Maybe he's got a reason. Why are they all here? This is a cruise, Seoras. Is he just picking off random people, posh people, people he doesn't like, or is there a good reason? Is there someone that these people have offended or done something to?

'I had thought of that,' said Macleod, 'and Ross is working on the connections.'

'The cabins, you found a cabin when he wasn't in. Maybe you can find the others, as he can't be in them all at once.'

'Leave that to me,' said Macleod. 'You need to go with the first officer and whoever else he gives you, and lie down.'

'Yes,' said the doctor. 'Lie down, get some water, get a cup of tea. Relax, let it go!'

Macleod watched as Jane was led away and saw her turn several times to look at him. He should have gone with her, but she had good people there. He didn't think she was in trouble. She'd wandered in on the killer. That was probably it. He hadn't asked how close the killer had got. It was the last thing she needed to do to remember. Instead, Macleod, making sure there was still an impromptu guard at the sauna, made his way up to the bridge. The Captain was sitting in his ready room.

'I've been informed, Seoras, that there's been another death.

'Your people have done well. Jane was attacked.'

'I heard that,' said the Captain. 'Fortunately, she escaped and I'm glad. If you want, I can put security around your cabin.'

'There's a couple of people there at the moment, I think that should suffice. I don't think he was coming after her. She walked in on something he'd just done. Professor Flores is dead.

'That's three,' said the Captain. 'I don't want to sound ungrateful, but how many more will there be? Is this going to continue?'

'I'm waiting for answers from the mainland. I'm waiting for connections. There's something I'd like to do in the meantime.'

Macleod explained about Jane's idea of the different disguises. The several cabins the killer might be using. Based on this, Macleod said he wanted to do a cabin lock-in. They would ask every passenger to remain in the cabin. The crew as well. A team of crewmates would then race around, making sure everyone was accounted for. They'd be able to spot the cabins nobody was inside of. Hence, they would then know the killer's extra personas.

'You're asking us to do something very public. So far, because the deaths have happened on the upper decks, we've been able to confine speculation to some people around there. We've kept most things quiet, as you asked, Inspector. This would seem to reverse that.'

'You're correct, and I appreciate what you're saying, but I

fell it needs to be done. I need to close this killer's exit routes. If we can make him stay in one persona, we'll have a better chance of finding him or her. Maybe you shouldn't suggest the cabin lock-in as some sort of action against a murderer. Maybe you tell the passengers you want to check that nobody's gone overboard.'

The Captain raised his eyebrows. 'Gone overboard, and yet we're not going back to look for them.'

'Say it happened a day or two ago. A person's missing,' said Macleod. 'That's the easiest way. Everybody in their cabins. I know there's a couple of thousand people on this boat, but it couldn't take more than an hour or two to achieve.'

'I'd hoped to keep this quiet, Inspector, but if you think it's for the best and it's what you need, then of course I'll do it. I will follow your instruction.'

'Thank you, Captain,' said Macleod. 'I need to come at this from two angles. I need to close where the killer can move to, and I need a team back on the mainland to come up with connections and get me the identity of who's doing this. How quick can you make this ship lock down happen?'

'I'll have it done in the next four hours. I just need to organise people and teams. There are certain crew who cannot leave post during this. Some are going to have to be working, but that's okay as long as they stay in the one place. We'll check everyone off. Don't worry.'

'Thank you,' said Macleod. He turned on his heel and left the bridge, striding back to see Jane at their cabin.

Three bodies, thought Macleod. *All killed in different ways. The link isn't how they died. The link must be the victims. Is it someone killing rich people? Why? There's no statement made against them. These people, if they knew who each other was, if they knew anything about why the killer was doing it, then maybe they'd hide that information.*

Macleod quickened his pace. He would narrow down the killer's options. Narrow down where he could operate out of. It was a start.

Chapter 15

Ross had driven through the night, racing down to Oxford. It had been a long haul. He'd stopped several times to take coffee on board while beside him on the front seat, various *munchy* items had come and gone.

As he arrived around about eight o'clock, the traffic was bad. Ross shook himself and fought his way through the traffic out to a rather pleasant village on the edge of Oxford. The road to it meandered with a quiet river snaking alongside.

John Surly's house could be seen as Ross approached it. A two-storey building with a widow's walk at the front. Considering the age, it seemed to be in remarkably good condition. The surrounding hedges were trimmed. The driveway was neat and as Ross pulled into it, he could see no sign of weeds through the gravel.

Ross stepped out of the car, allowed himself a little shake and the cooler air to revive him. Ross prided himself on being extremely professional and so he did up his tie, put on his jacket, and walked to the front door. There was a doorbell, which he pressed, and he could hear the corresponding ring in the background.

Nothing moved within the house. Ross pressed the button

again. Again, nothing moved. Next, Ross tried the large knocker, hitting it so hard that he thought he could have woken half the neighbourhood but, again, there was no response. Ross took a walk around the outside of the building, looking inside where he could. Most of the curtains seemed drawn, but the few that weren't showed an immaculate house. One that Ross thought wasn't lived in but was maintained.

As he spun around looking at the gardens and the house, everything looked so perfect. Is that who John Surly was? Was he a man of perfection? Was he a man who liked things to be just so? Ross decided to try the neighbour and walked out of the driveway. He took a left into the driveway of Surly's neighbour.

The corresponding driveway, although it looked like the same gravel and the same length, had a large number of weeds growing through it. The house, a similar shape to Surly's, but with no widow's walk, was certainly not in the same condition as Surly's. A cast iron drainpipe was hanging off the rear and the front garden had many toys strewn across it.

Ross smiled. Since having his own child, he had a more relaxed attitude about how neat everything should be kept. While he maintained his pristine shirt and tie for his job, at home, he was much more casual, finding himself too tired to care. How things had changed.

As Ross wandered down the driveway, he heard some shouting from inside the house. At first, his ears pricked up but then he relaxed, realising it was a mother shouting at children to hurry up. *It must be about school time*, he thought and quickened his pace to the front door.

He pressed the doorbell and couldn't hear a sound inside. He looked for the knocker. There had been one on the door before, for he saw the holes it had been attached by. Ross lifted his hand and rapped the door as best he could. There came no response but more shouting upstairs, so Ross knocked again. This time, the door was opened, and a small face looked up at him.

'Hello, I am Detective Constable Ross. I've travelled a long way to meet the man next door, but I'd like to talk to your parents or whoever looks after you.'

The young boy looked up at him and gave a cheeky grin. He turned around and shouted, 'Mum', before turning back, looking up at Ross. Ross smiled back and the boy smiled again. There was a sound of feet thundering down the stairs and then a shout of, 'Who is it?'

The child turned and raised his shoulders, indicating he didn't know.

'I'm Detective Constable Ross.'

'Well, you've picked a bloody awful time to come.'

'I apologise. I've come all the way from Inverness.'

The door opened, and a woman stood in a dressing gown. Her hair was a mess, and she turned and shouted up the stairs, calling out three children's names.

'Like I say, it's not a good time, but given where you've come from, I guess you will not be coming back.'

'Well, I'm not here for you,' said Ross. 'I'm here for next door, John Surly. That is where he lives, isn't it?'

'Him? Yes, that's where he lives.'

'Something wrong with him?' asked Ross.

'Mr Bloody Perfect complains about the kids a lot. Anyway, I haven't seen him. I don't see him. He keeps himself to himself. I don't know why he's got that garden.'

'Looks like he does a lot of work in it,' said Ross.

'Oh, he doesn't. Gets somebody else to do it. Likes things spic and span. Every time he's come in here or looked over, I can hear him tutting. He's no idea what it's like running a house full of kids. Do you?'

'Yes, I do,' said Ross. 'Got one of my own now.'

'Well, try five,' said the woman. 'Anyway, I've got to get them out to school. Anything else I can help you with?'

'Yes, how long has it been since you saw him next door?'

'Oh, several days at least.'

'How often would you see him?'

'Usually, once a day. I see him going in and out. Is the car there?'

'No,' said Ross.

'He parks his car on the drive. The one without the weeds, as he told me once.'

'I've got the feeling you two don't get on.'

'I get on fine with people. I don't need them telling me my business.'

'Fair enough,' said Ross. 'You haven't seen him for several days. It's not normal, and the car is not there. That's what you're telling me.'

'Yes,' said the woman.

'Well, thank you for your time. I'll let you get on.'

Ross turned and walked back out of the driveway riddled with weeds. He stopped himself from thinking ill of Surly. Just because a man liked to be tidy didn't mean there was something particularly bad about him. Just because he didn't like weeds, or he paid someone to do his garden, didn't make him evil. However, what bothered Ross was the man hadn't been seen.

Ross thought back to his notes on Surly. When he looked for the man, he was still working up at the university. He was sure he'd seen that. It was worth a punt before he went anywhere else. Ross walked back down Surly's drive and then stood beside his car, taking out his mobile phone. He rang the university switchboard and asked for John Surly.

'Do you know which department he works in?'

'I'm not sure,' said Ross. 'He originally had been in the English department, but it's been a long time since.'

Ross didn't want to push people down channels and thought it better to let them do a little digging work.

'Give me a moment,' said the man.

Ross tapped his foot and looked around. He didn't like it. The house seemed quiet. He walked up to the front door, pushed open the letterbox, and looked in. He couldn't see down to the floor. If there were letters down there, that would show that there was a problem, or that the man was simply away. Ross couldn't see anything. He wandered around the side of the house before he heard the phone again.

'I think he's in the English department,' said the switchboard operator. 'I'll put you through and see what's what.'

'Thank you,' said Ross, and stood, waiting to be connected through.

'English department,' said the voice.

'Hello, I'm Detective Constable Ross and I am looking for John Surly. Does he work there?'

'He does some part-time work with us, and usually pops in three, four times a week. He's got an office of his own, but John doesn't keep regular hours, though, so I don't know if he's in or not. If you hold on for a moment, I'll go find out.'

Ross said he would wait and then he walked further around the back of the house. The river he'd seen previously when driving into the village snaked along the back of Surly's house.

He stared at its meandering. The air was cool, still that winter feel about it, and he could see little around the river. The trees that shrouded it made it a dark retreat from the main road. Much more so than the better-lit house.

'Hello,' said the voice on the other end of the phone.

'Yes, I'm still here,' said Ross.

'I've gone looking for John Surly. He's not in his office, so I asked a few of the other professors and some of the staff. He hasn't been seen for several days.'

'Right,' said Ross. 'Is that normal?'

'He keeps himself to himself with the work he does. He doesn't need to be in except for the occasional meeting. If he's gone somewhere, it wouldn't really bother any of the staff.'

'Do you know what car he drives?' asked Ross.

'Yes, it's the old brown banger. Well, it's not a banger. If you'd tell him that, he'd chew your face off.'

'Why?' asked Ross.

'He says it's a collector's item. I know the car. I don't know what type of car it is. Morris? I don't know. Something like that.'

'Would you recognise it?' asked Ross.

'Yes, I would.'

'I appreciate this is taking up your time, but it is important. Can I ask that you look in the car parks around where John would normally park and see if Surly's car is there? I'm currently standing at his house and it's not here.'

'Well, if he's been away, he'd probably have the car with him.'

'I appreciate that, but I just want to confirm that the car is not at the university.'

'I don't really see how it would be,' said the voice on the other end.

'Please indulge me,' said Ross. 'I just have to confirm things sometimes.'

More than that, thought Ross, *if it is there, I'm driving up to the university to find him. This will save me from a wasted trip.*

Ross waited again, trying to peer past more of the curtains of the house, but couldn't see anything. The chill in the air was getting to him now. It had livened him up previously, but it was now making him want to retreat into his own car.

'Hello there,' said the voice again. 'No, he's not here. The car's not here at all.'

'Sorry for wasting your time,' said Ross, 'but that is helpful. Thank you.'

Ross looked around for a moment. There was a small garage at the end of the driveway. He couldn't see into it as it had wooden doors that closed across the front completely. There was a padlock on the outside. He saw a side door as well.

Ross looked first at the garage. Going up to the glass-fronted main doors, he gave them a wipe with his sleeve, cursing the dirt that came off the window onto it. He peered inside. There was a brown shape in there. *That's a car,* he thought. *That's a brown car, and it's his. And it's here. No wonder he hasn't been heard of.*

Ross went up to the side door in the garage and realised it was locked. He was concerned. There were two dead on the boat. Surly was part of the group. Ross went back to his own car, took a crowbar out of the boot and came back to the door in the garage. He pulled at it, jimmying the door open against the rather insignificant lock.

Ross stepped inside and saw the brown car previously described to him. It took him a moment to open the car door, which wasn't locked. He searched the car and inside the rest of the garage. There was no one there.

Ross then made his way to the back door of the house. It was an old-style door and, again, he could jimmy it open with the crowbar. Once inside the house, it took Ross a full ten minutes to walk around it, searching cupboards, wardrobes, anywhere the man might be. He even went up into the roof space.

Ross came down and walked out through the door at the back. He was about to phone the Oxford Police to advise them what he'd done, in case anybody reported damage at the house. When he looked down towards the river, a chill came across Ross.

If you wanted something to be quiet, if you wanted to get rid of someone? he mused.

Ross walked down the rear garden of the house. There was a large hedge around it, but at the end where the river was, it was lower. He could see the far side of the river. The top of the garden was higher up, but it then slid down and the entire width of the river came into view. It wasn't particularly wide, but wider than most streams that ran behind houses.

Looking left and right, Ross saw where it had fattened out. Ross stood on the edge of the makeshift riverbank. He had to be careful in case he slipped down into the water. He looked up and along the banks.

If you wanted to get rid of someone, he thought, *this would be a good place. The river meandered on up behind the houses, but Surly's house was one of the few that seemed to have access out to the river.*

There were trees along the bank he was standing on, except for the back of Surly's house. Ross crouched down, looking left and right along the far bank, and then he checked the bank he was standing on. There were some scraggly bushes well beyond Surly's lawn. As he approached one of them, Ross looked down at the grass and saw a rope.

It looked like a tow rope, the sort you would use for a car. It was blue, not overly thick, but certainly strong enough. He ran his hands along it and found it tied around the root of one of the bushes on the bank.

Ross traced it the other way and found it disappearing into the water. Maybe it was from a boat. Maybe the boat had sunk. Ross grabbed the rope and pulled at it. It seemed tight. He gave another pull before taking off his jacket and tie and laying them down to one side. Ross pulled again, digging his feet into the bank.

Suddenly, the rope gave way, causing him to fall onto his backside. Ross pulled at it again as he got up to his feet and slowly, the rope came closer. He saw something break the surface of the water and suddenly, everything became heavier. Ross pulled hard and saw a man-sized figure with a rope tied around it coming up onto the bank.

Ross tried not to focus on the figure but pulled with all his might until it had cleared the river. Slowly, he walked over and looked down. Ross was no expert in forensics, but this body had been in the river for a while at least.

He picked up his phone, dialled 999, and asked for the attendance of the Oxford Police. He gave his rank and who he was and said he'd just found a body. After closing the call down, Ross stood looking down at the man before him.

He'd seen a photograph of Surly. *Yes*, he thought, *that's probably him. Rather than upset any of the local police*, he thought, *I'll wait for them before searching the body*.

Ross walked up the bank and continued up towards the

driveway. He could just about see where the body was at this point, and he could see if anyone was coming towards it. If the police arrived, they would see him in the driveway.

He called the Inverness office, and the call was picked up by Cunningham.

'Ross,' she said, 'how's things?'

'Body found,' he said simply. 'I think it's Surly. I don't know and I'm not sure. This thing's growing arms and legs, or bodies at least.'

Chapter 16

Clarissa Urquhart drove off the ferry at Craignure, looking to head towards Tobermory. Filton Pritchard had an address there, a small art shop along the front among the multi-coloured buildings that made Tobermory so famous. It was a small shop as far as she knew, his main stock being held elsewhere within a warehouse.

Although he was retired, it was believed that someone else had picked up his business. Filton was around the area, possibly advising but not carrying out the day-to-day activities. If he was on the island, Clarissa would find him.

It was strange being hauled back in to work with the team just as she had got established in the arts team. She had left Paterson trying to acclimatise to life in the arts world. He was a quick learner, but he was extremely green. Still, she had a soft spot for him.

He had overcome his embarrassment about the cut around his neck. She had stopped staring at it, too. It had got so bad at first that she'd bought him a cravat to wear. When he started to look like a theatre lovey, it was quite funny, because he was polite, but didn't speak like a lovey. It had stopped Clarissa from looking at him and seeing imaginary blood pouring out.

Her hand had covered the wound. She had kept him alive, and it seemed that the pair of them seemed tied by that twist of fate. She would get him back to being the officer he once was and if he didn't, she'd find him a way of living, a place in the world, be that in the police world or not. He'd taken an incredible hit, and so had she, but maybe her healing was also in his.

Clarissa swerved suddenly, avoiding a car that was on the correct side of the road, her little green one having drifted across. She hadn't slept well the night before, stopping in a B&B before getting the ferry as early as she could. Now, in what would be described as the normal hours of morning, she was driving over towards Tobermory in a jaded state.

As she joined the tight road that then hooked round and down onto the shorefront of coloured buildings, she thought Tobermory was a grand place to live. Clarissa liked colour; she liked something different, for she was different, and tough as nails. She also had a love for the finer things in life. Unpredictable, resilient and yet spontaneous—that was Clarissa, even if she said so herself. Yes, Paterson was lucky.

Macleod, on the other hand, was typical Macleod. Wherever the man went, there was a case. Dead bodies followed him. She hoped this wouldn't be the case with Filton Pritchard. She'd had enough dead bodies to do her the rest of her life, especially those—she didn't think about those though, did she? Not the children. That was really what had done it. The children who had died. Adult bodies were not pleasant, but she could handle that. The children, not so.

Clarissa parked her little green sports car and wandered along the seafront until she came to a smallish building. It said 'Antiques' over the top and as she looked in the window,

Clarissa re-described it as junk. Regardless, she flung her shawl over her shoulder, marched in her tartan trews and bid a fond 'good day' to the woman behind the counter.

'Clarissa Urquhart,' said Clarissa. 'I was looking to see if you had something special, not the tat in the window.'

'Right,' said the younger woman. 'Any line you were looking for, or any particular period?'

'Something not far off when I was born,' said Clarissa. 'Goes by the name of Filton Pritchard.'

'Filton's on holiday.'

'And you might be?'

'Ellie. Ellie Moffat.'

'Well, Ellie, any idea when Filton will be back?'

'It's going to be several weeks at least.'

'All right. Where's he gone?'

'He went cruising,' said Ellie suddenly.

'Anywhere in particular?'

'Just one of those large boats.'

'Any particular company?' persisted Clarissa.

'I don't know. Might have been one of those TV company ones, whatever you call them, or the Norwegian guy. Something or other.'

'He go on his own?'

'Yes, he did. Keen to see the world.'

Keen to see the world on a cruise? thought Clarissa. *All you see is the sea and a couple of shows at night and get fed so much, you're stuffed as anything. Different if you went north, and maybe see the icebergs or the glaciers, and all that stuff.*

'I'm Detective Inspector Clarissa Urquhart,' said Clarissa. 'I need to speak to Filton. Would you have a number for him?'

'No, I don't, actually. I don't have his mobile. I think he

changed it recently.'

The girl seemed agitated. Clarissa put her age at around twenty-five.

'Well, where do you live?' asked Clarissa.

'Oh, I have a room in Filton's house. He's got like a bedsit bit. It came with the job. Handy for the both of us.'

Clarissa nodded and looked around. 'If you hear from him,' she said, 'Get him to contact me.' Clarissa handed over her card. 'Clarissa Urquhart, you've probably heard of me. I am reasonably well known in the arts world.'

'Of course,' said the girl. Clarissa turned to walk out, then looked up at a painting. 'How much are you asking for that?'

'Two hundred,' said the girl. 'It's because of the period it's from.'

Clarissa walked over, and picked up a card underneath. *17th century. 17th century?* She examined it carefully. *20th more like.* She turned with the card and put it down in front of the girl.

'Go round and redo your cards because some of these, frankly, are bollocks.'

Her language caught the girl off guard, and Clarissa almost laughed. 'Tell Filton to contact me if you hear from him. When you do hear from him, tell him also that when I come back, I expect everything in this shop to be advertised correctly. He's a dealer and I know he knows his stuff. Why is he bothering to try to make off the punter?'

The girl rolled her shoulders nervously and looked away from Clarissa. 'If he contacts me,' she said.

Clarissa slammed her hand down on the counter.

'When he contacts you. This is his business? No? Or is it yours?'

'I'm running it, but he's sort of looking after it.'

139

'So, you're doing the front work? Very good. He's the guy behind it. It's his business. Like I said, when he gets in contact.' Clarissa slammed her fist down in time with the words, 'You and he contact me!'

She turned on her heel and glided out of the building. She turned left and walked along until she found an ice cream shop. It was cold outside, with a piercing chill in the air, but Clarissa liked ice cream. A '99' as well. It was mint chocolate chip with a waffle cone and a flake sticking out of the top of it.

Clarissa walked back towards the shop, but not into the direct line of the window. A little down from it, where she sat eating her ice cream. It took a while before she realised Filton wasn't coming out. He probably wasn't in there then.

She got into her car and drove along a little and parked it up so she could keep warm inside. Clarissa had her lunch, a mid-afternoon snack, and her dinner in the car, and chips to finish. It was seven o'clock that night before Ellie left the building.

In the meantime, Ross had contacted her telling her of the demise of John Surly, or at least the suspected body of John Surly. Clarissa wondered had Ellie done for Filton Pritchard.

She watched Ellie walk down the street. Clarissa sat and watched the cars coming back along. There was no other way out by road, and sure enough, soon a small Micra drove past her and Clarissa spun out a little behind it. The Micra went to the end of the street, turned up the hill, parked up at the supermarket, and Clarissa watched Ellie get out. She came back with a couple of bottles of wine and what looked like enough food for at least two people.

Ellie then drove a little out of Tobermory before turning off at a cottage. She parked up in the driveway and Clarissa noticed there was already a car there. Parking at the end of the drive looking down, Clarissa saw Ellie get out, take her shopping in through the front door, closing it behind her.

Clarissa parked her car up, got out, threw the shawl around her, and marched down the driveway. There was something about Ellie. She was nervous when Clarissa spoke to her, but then again, Clarissa was used to that. She made many people nervous, but there was something else in the answers that were given. Clarissa didn't believe for one minute that Filton wasn't around.

Walking up the driveway, she tried to stay quiet, and instead of going to the door, she slunk around the side of the cottage. Cautiously, she peered in through a window.

Ellie was putting a bottle of wine on the table. There was another bottle as well. One red, one white. Unless you were holding a dinner party, that was an awful lot for one person. It was even a lot for two, unless one didn't like the other. She watched Ellie take off her coat, standing in jeans and a long jumper. Then an older man approached her.

His hands went round, firmly grasping her backside and pulling her towards him. The woman seemed quite happy with this, and they kissed long and deep. Clarissa had seen younger photos of Filton Pritchard, but none as he was now. She turned and marched round to the front door. There was a knocker at the top and she banged on it like she was trying to wake the dead.

There was a delay and Clarissa thought about rapping on the door again, but that would give away somebody being urgent if he didn't want to be discovered. So, she considered her options for a moment. She walked to the side of the cottage, looked in, and then looked to the other side. There was another cottage just to the right, and Clarissa saw a small gate and a hedge at the rear of both buildings. She turned and banged on the door again, satisfied with what would happen.

Ellie Moffat answered the door about thirty seconds later. She looked flushed, and then she saw it was Clarissa.

'Detective Sergeant Urquhart.'

'Detective Inspector Urquhart, actually. I want to speak to Filton.'

'I told you; Filton is not here.'

'You drink a lot of wine, do you? That's a bit much, and is Filton all right with the older guy you've got in the house?'

Ellie looked astonished. Her eyes cast to the left. Clarissa turned and ran hard down the driveway. She turned at the end towards the driveway of the house next door and saw a shadow about to emerge from it. She stuck out her foot, and a man tripped over it, sprawling onto the ground. Clarissa walked quickly over and put her foot on his back.

'Don't kill me,' said the man. 'Please, don't kill me. I'm unarmed. Don't kill me.'

'Why would I want to kill you? I'm Detective Inspector Clarissa Urquhart. Apart from the fact that you're selling some very dodgy gear in your shop, I just want to speak to you. You are Filton Pritchard, are you not?'

Ellie Moffat came running up the driveway, holding a rolling pin in her hand.

'You get off him. Leave him alone. Don't kill him.'

'I'm not killing anyone,' said Clarissa, but Ellie Moffat charged at her, anyway. Clarissa stepped to one side, kicked the woman hard in the shins, and she collapsed down to the ground. The rolling pin hit the ground too, falling from Ellie's hand, and it bounced away to one side.

'Can we stop?' asked Clarissa. 'Can we just stop? Because the next time one of you two comes at me, I will hit back hard. Listen, very carefully. I am Detective Inspector Clarissa Urquhart, and I am not here to kill you. I am here to talk about the Dead Rubber Society.'

'The what?' blurted Ellie.

'He knows,' said Clarissa.

Clarissa returned her foot to the man's back as he tried to turn over to talk to her, and she kept it there.

'It wasn't me. It's Surly. Surly did it all. Surly was the man who did everything. You want Surly. Don't kill me.'

'I'm the police,' said Clarissa. She reached inside her shawl and pulled out her ID, shoving it down towards the man. 'Police, Detective Inspector, I'm not a hit woman. Do I look like a hit woman? What hit woman turns up in tartan trews and a shawl? They'd spot me a mile away.'

The man's face suddenly seemed to show some relief. 'Thank goodness,' he said. 'They're coming for us. I'm sure of it. Somebody needs to warn Surly. I tried to warn him.'

'John Surly's dead,' said Clarissa. 'Died in Oxford. I think you and I need to have a conversation. My boss has got bodies on a boat and he thinks there's going to be more. When I take my foot off your back, you'll stand up and we'll go back into the house. Understood?'

Filton nodded. Clarissa let her foot off his back, and he stood up and dusted himself down.

'Slowly, back to the house,' said Clarissa. Beside her, Ellie Moffat stood up and went to walk past her, but Clarissa put her hand in front of her.

'You ever come at me with a rolling pin again and I'll brain you with it. We don't take that sort of nonsense. Now get in that house and shut up when I talk to him. Oh, and by the way, Pritchard, what age?'

Pritchard didn't turn walking back to the house.

'Age doesn't matter,' said Ellie.

'That's what my twenty-year-old lover tells me,' laughed Clarissa, and stomped off down the driveway behind the other two.

Chapter 17

The mood of the passengers, possibly all two thousand of them, was very much against Macleod's decision at that point. They didn't know that he'd specifically asked for it, but they were about to undergo a cabin-wide lockdown. It would only be for about three hours, but most were complaining. Why couldn't they do it in the middle of the night, or certainly in the early hours in the morning? Find a time when everybody didn't want to be doing things on their holiday.

Macleod, however, wanted it done as soon as possible. The trouble was, the killer had struck, and if they intended to kill several people, they would try to do it quickly. After all, the longer they stayed on the vessel, the longer they continued to operate, the greater likelihood they could get caught. With the vessel due into port in the next couple of days, time was running out for Macleod.

Jane asked if she could accompany Macleod as the lockdown took place, and after the time she'd just had, Macleod thought it was wise.

'Stick with me and stay close. However, if we have to go into a room and there's any danger, you'll be going to stand with some of the crew elsewhere.'

'Of course, Seoras,' said Jane. 'I just don't want to be stuck in the cabin on my own. I don't think it's safe.'

'I don't think he'll be coming after you.'

'Why?' asked Jane.

'From what you described to me, coming out of the sauna, he would've had the perfect opportunity to despatch you, but he fled. He obviously wasn't worried that you'd seen him.'

'Because I haven't. I can't tell you anything about him. Just it seemed like a man.'

'I wonder if he knows that. Either way, though, of course, you can stay close. Just be prepared to be told to stand back if things get a little ropey.'

Macleod took Jane up to the bridge of the vessel when the lockdown began. The Captain remained on the bridge, but most of his officers and a lot of his crew were out and about. Not only were the passengers being vetted, but the crew were as well, most of them confined to quarters, except for those who had to be on station. The entertainment people, those who serviced the cabins, those who looked after the passengers on board, were mostly in their quarters. Those who ran the ship as a vessel were helping with the search or maintaining their duty.

The search would take time, and this frustrated Macleod because he was stuck up on the bridge with nothing to do. Jane, however, stood looking out of the front of the vessel, the Captain beside her.

'It's quite the view,' he said. 'Even better when we get closer to land. Have you recovered from your ordeal?'

'It's not the worst one I've suffered,' said Jane, causing the Captain to raise his eyebrows. He turned and looked at

Macleod. Seoras simply gave a nod. Being a partner of, or married to, a police officer often exposed you to bad things. In Jane's case, they were highly physical, which was uncommon. For others, however, the emotional trauma that was brought home often stayed with the partner as well.

Macleod was disappointed that it had followed them out here. This was their time away. Time for Jane and him to relax. He'd look to claim the time back whenever he got home because he was working. He'd take her away again, maybe another cruise, if she wanted it.

There was a call from one of the officers on the bridge, saying it was for the Captain. He picked up one of the phones on the bridge station, gave several nods, then put it back down again.

'The second officer here will take you down. We found a cabin that's empty. Apparently, it should be occupied by two men. They'll have the details down at the cabin.'

Macleod turned on his heel, and Jane went to follow him.

'You're welcome to stay here,' said the Captain.

'No,' said Jane. 'I'll be with my Seoras. I'll be fine with him.'

'Thank you, Captain,' said Macleod, 'but I still need Jane. She's my right hand at the moment.'

Together, they marched quickly along the various corridors and down to a lower deck and an inner cabin. Standing outside was a crew member in a white shirt.

'Detective Chief Inspector Macleod,' said Seoras, coming up to the man and shaking his hand. 'What have you got for me?'

'Can't get an answer from this cabin. Tried ringing the bell, tried banging on the door, nothing.'

'Who is in here?'

'Two men, both Scottish. McTaggart and McPherson.'

'Okay, can we look inside?'

'The Captain has okayed it,' said the man, and took a key card, pressing it up against the sensor. The door clicked open, and Macleod slowly pushed the door back. Interior cabins were tiny compared to his own.

Walking in, he saw two beds, one on either side. The bunks above them were not pulled down but left up on their side. He turned and opened up a couple of cupboards and found some bags. The little en suite had toothpaste in it, brushes, but there was not a lot of distress to the cabin. He turned back to the beds. They were immaculate, not slept in.

Following him in, Jane looked around. 'It's not quite the same as the other one you found, is it?' she said.

'No.' Macleod stepped out of the cabin, turned to the man there, and asked him to seal it and place someone on duty in front of it. If anyone was to try and go back in, Macleod was to be contacted immediately at the bridge. Returning to the bridge, Macleod used one of the satellite phones to call Hope in Inverness. It was currently in the evening in Scotland.

'What can we do for you, wanderer?' asked Hope on the phone.

'McTaggart and McPherson,' said Macleod. 'I'm going to email you some details on them. I believe we may have a copy of passports as well. I need you to do a search. Tell me who they are.'

'I'll be back to you within about half an hour,' said Hope.

Macleod walked to the front of the boat where the sunshine was blasting in through the wide windows.

'Do you think this is something?' the Captain asked him.

'No,' said Macleod firmly. 'I don't think it's anything that's a police matter. It might be a matter for you, depending on what's happening.'

'How do you mean?' asked the Captain.

'The bed's not slept in. That means that our two men may be elsewhere. I don't know how you view that sort of thing, or what's allowed or not.'

'Lighten up, Seoras,' said Jane. 'You were lucky you were just too old at the time I got hold of you. Any younger, we'd have been doing the same.'

Macleod raised his eyebrows and thought he heard the Captain snigger. He turned and walked past Jane, and quietly whispered in her ear, 'but we wouldn't have to tell everyone about it.'

Before Hope had called back, the bridge received another call, and Macleod was shown down to another cabin. It was an interior one, two decks below the previous one, and inside sat two men and two women. The men were sitting in T-shirts, boxer shorts, and the women had dressing gowns from the ship wrapped around them.

'Let me guess,' said Macleod, walking in, 'McTaggart and McPherson?'

'We have done nothing wrong,' said the man. 'We were just—'

'Just taking the opportunity for some alone time,' said Jane.

Macleod turned to the women, and asked for their passports. They handed them over. He took a note of the numbers and then handed them back.

'Just remain here for the meantime,' said Macleod. 'The next time you're asked to go to your cabins, go to the right ones, please. Or at the very least, put somebody in each of them.'

He started out of the cabin, with Jane close behind him. As they walked on their way back up to the bridge, Macleod could feel her wanting to say something.

'What?' he said, as they got into the lift for the upper decks.

She put her arm on his shoulder. 'You know something, it's quite, well, romantic, I guess.'

'What was?'

'Both in the same cabin.'

'Don't,' said Macleod.

'Don't what?'

'Don't go off on some little tease.'

'Bit kinky, really, isn't it?'

'I've got enough on my plate,' said Macleod. 'We don't need to be discussing this sort of thing.'

She threw her arms around him, pulling him close. 'I come away with you to get some time together, and we get a case.'

'I got a case,' said Macleod. 'You're just helping me.'

'I know. Finally, we get a period when you're not thinking, when you're not engaged in it all.'

'I'm always thinking,' said Macleod. He felt her hands run across his chest. She kissed him behind the ear.

'You know I lose you at times, don't you?'

'You don't lose me,' said Macleod.

'Oh, I do. There's this other woman. There's this other person in your life. You go off to work and she takes over. She dominates you. She owns you during that time.'

Macleod looked hurt. 'I will admit, the first time I met Hope, I struggled with her. I struggled with feelings, but I haven't felt like that in a long time. Hope doesn't dominate me.'

'Seoras, you're such an idiot,' said Jane. 'Good job I love you.'

Macleod looked at her quizzically.

'It's the force, the case, being a detective. Crime. That's the one you dance your little dances with. That's the one who sucks you in and wraps her arms around you. Call it a case, whatever. Numerous women. Each one slightly different.

That's who takes you away from me. That's where I lose out.'

Macleod turned and put his hand up. 'Sorry,' he said, 'It's who I am.'

'I know, and I love you for it, but I actually thought we might get some time, being away from Inverness, being out of reach of the station.'

'I'll make it up to you.'

'Don't promise. I'm okay, Seoras. I just want this done as quick as possible.'

'Me too,' said Macleod.

Before they'd reached the bridge, the second officer had come looking for them, for another empty cabin had been found. Macleod was taken to one in the lower decks, which belonged to a couple. It looked similar to the one he'd searched not that long ago, except, when he opened up every drawer, every cupboard, and looked inside, there were no items. The cabin was completely bare. It belonged to a couple. A couple no one had seen.

'They have passport numbers, don't they?' asked Macleod. He knew he'd have to get those from the ship's records. There were two other cabins found, both single male travellers. Both cabins were completely empty. The ages of the missing passengers varied by about twenty years. None of them could be found.

There were hints they'd popped in. The door access said they'd been in, but not for several days. Macleod brought the neighbours of the cabins together, asked when they'd seen them. But beyond a brief initial meeting, during which those who occupied the cabin did everything they could not to show their faces, there had been no sightings. Even with the couple, no woman had been seen.

151

Macleod and Jane sat down with the Captain in his ready room after the lockdown had been lifted. There were four people not accounted for, all with empty cabins.

'How did they get on board?' asked Macleod.

'All came on at different ports.'

'So, someone has come off and come back on as someone else,' said Macleod.

'It looks like it,' said the Captain. 'Their first access is at different times. Come on, got that cabin, then moved on to the next one.'

'So we know,' said Macleod, 'that our passenger, our killer, has been on for a while.'

'He's been on for over a week,' said the Captain. 'Unfortunately, that will not help you a lot.'

'Why?' asked Macleod.

'Well, you think he's male? That's fine, but we've got over two thousand passengers. If you take the male ones, we've got eleven hundred. Those who have been on for over a week, nine hundred.'

'I'm afraid that's not just it, though,' said Macleod. 'There's no reason it can't be one of your crew.' The Captain looked up.

'Why can't they pop off, come back on? They know how this place works. What bothers me is, has he deliberately made them come here?'

'How does he get everybody here?' asked Jane.

'That's the trick,' said Macleod, 'isn't it? You could go elsewhere. You could kill somebody, but here, you can disappear amongst thousands of people. Here, you can be somebody else. Here, if discovered, he can set himself up to become someone else. All these alibis, all these other people he can be.'

'They are all on open dining options as well. Nothing where you book the table. You just go in,' said the Captain. 'That was clever.'

'Where have we got to,' said Macleod. 'Having done this, where are we at?'

'Well,' said Jane, 'he's got nowhere to hide anymore, has he?'

'No,' said Macleod, but he looked glum.

'That's a good thing though, isn't it?' said the Captain.

'Well, it is,' said Jane. 'He can't just disappear.'

'No,' said Macleod, 'he can't, but what we've done is trap him. We've got a couple more days at sea at most. Whatever else he's going to do, whatever other killings he needs to do, they're going to get done now, and I think he'll do them as quick as he can. We're in not a great situation. I need to find who he is.'

'We could search all the cabins.'

'What do you mean?' asked Macleod. 'We've just gone through everyone.'

'I have the power. I can enable you to search every cabin.'

'And how many cabins is that, Captain? Best part of a thousand? The manpower to do it? We'd have to search all the cabins from the crew as well. Once he knows we started searching, it'll be dead easy to get rid of any evidence. That's if he hasn't done it already, over the side.

'No,' said Macleod. 'We will discover who he is. Do good old-fashioned detective work back on the mainland. I'm going to talk to Hope about the passports and get an update on what's going on with Clarissa and Ross. John Surly's dead, but Ross might track something back from that. I know Clarissa has found Filton Pritchard,' he said to Jane. 'Let's see what she can get out of him.'

Chapter 18

The living room of Filton Pritchard had a large stove in it, and the burning logs generated such a heat that even Clarissa was feeling warm. She'd taken off her large shawl, hanging it over a chair, daring anyone to try sitting on it. She pulled a separate chair over for herself and told Pritchard and Ellie Moffat to sit opposite her. Clarissa wanted to watch the reaction on both faces, as stories were told. They were nervous, extremely so.

'Something's clearly up,' said Clarissa. 'You were worried I'm going to kill you. I kept telling you I'm a detective. I'm a police officer. You're still a tad worried that I'm going to kill you. You've really got the spooks, Filton. Do you want to tell me why?'

The man looked away. 'It's just an old thing. Just some nutters.'

'I think it's more than nutters,' said Clarissa. 'People don't disappear, not to be in their shop, not to be around the area they're from just because of some nutters. You're worried that I was going to come and kill you, but look at me. You seriously think I kill people?'

Filton looked up at Ellie, and Clarissa didn't see any belief in their eyes that she couldn't kill them.

'The fewer people know about this, the better,' said Filton suddenly.

'I'm the police,' said Clarissa. 'Do you get that? Detective inspector, and you will tell me what's going on.'

The man looked away suddenly. Clarissa stood up. She never had great height, but she cut an imposing figure when she got up close to you. She always thought it was the unpredictability of what she was going to do.

When she'd been a young officer, a sergeant had told her to keep people on their toes, and she'd taken it to heart. He'd also taught her how to fight dirty. The key, he said, was not to be the better fighter, to be the one who could stand tall, the one who had all the techniques. The key thing was to be standing at the end.

Never doing anything underhand meant that you had to go the long way around. You had to be the one who took the shortcut and be there first.

Clarissa stood in the face of Filton Pritchard and said nothing until he turned and looked into her eyes.

'Mr Pritchard, the Dead Rubber society. Tell me all and tell me now, or I will lift you, and haul you into whatever station they've got here, and then I'll haul you over to the mainland. I'm in the middle of a murder investigation. Yes, a murder investigation and I'm probably your best option to end this without you ending up in a body bag somewhere.'

It was probably over the top. He could run away and hide in some other fashion, but Clarissa could see he was shaking. Ellie Moffat beside him was, too.

'Okay,' he said. 'Okay. Look, it was all back in the Oxford days.'

'So I hear,' said Clarissa. 'Go on.'

'There was an Oxford don, and he left behind a fortune, but he was a nasty bugger with it. You see, there was a group of six that he invited for the money, but he said that only five of them could get it.

'Was there anyone else involved' asked Clarissa, 'because forgive me, you don't look like you've got a lot of money?'

'I wasn't one of the six,' said Filton. I was the one who administered the money.'

'Just you?'

'No. John Surly as well.'

'So, you two gave the money out?'

'Yes,' said Filton. 'The Oxford don died, and in his will, he left behind this money. It stipulated the terms in the will, and we got a separate letter from his solicitor to say what we were to do. Definite instructions. We were given a small remuneration for it, too small a remuneration for it. He had picked out six men, and in truth, I think they were up-and-coming students who were of the entrepreneurial bent. I believe the idea was that the money was going to help them, but one of them wasn't going to get it. The don was trying to put a bit of steam in some of them. I don't know. Either way, it was a nasty piece of work.'

'Well, tell me about the process,' said Clarissa.

'Well, he picked out these six men.'

'And one of the names was Warren Kilmartin,' said Clarissa.

Filton looked a little shocked. 'Yes, it is.'

'Another person was Professor Flores.'

'I don't know if he's a professor or not, but Carlos Flores—he was one of the other ones.'

'And a David Durston,' said Clarissa.

157

'That's right. There was Durston as well. How did you know?'

'Because those people are dead,' said Clarissa. 'I told you I'm investigating murders. Who else was involved?'

'Fergus Verde and Johan Risenberger,' said Filton. 'And there was also a Miles Lafferty.'

'So how did it work?' asked Clarissa.

'Well, the instruction had been given that they were to play cards. Five of them were to go away with money, but, of course, he didn't say it was equal money. It was depending on how you played. They were basically going to keep playing until one person had gone bankrupt. At that point, everybody else took the money they had won.'

'Well, it seems straightforward. What went wrong?' asked Clarissa.

'Warren Kilmartin came to me. He'd been talking with some of the others. The problem was that Miles Lafferty was a card shark, and he was a damn good one. I think our friend, the Oxford don, put him in there deliberately. I think he was trying to teach them that business life was tough, and sometimes, you had to not play by the rules if you wanted to get on. The sums of money were significant, several hundred thousand. Good for start-up, good for getting you going in your business. Surly and I, we were only going to get about five hundred pounds each for setting this up. However, Kilmartin came to us, and he said we would get significantly more.'

'How much more?'

'Ten thousand each, but we had to rig the game.'

'Rig it?'

'Very much so,' said Filton. 'We had to rig the cards. The trouble was, Lafferty was good, and he would know, but if we

158

were all there, he couldn't do anything about it. He could call cheat, but, of course, Surly and I were there to verify the result. We were the ones giving out the money. We were the ones going to sign it off.'

'Doesn't look like you made a brilliant decision on that one,' said Carissa, 'given your current circumstances. How did it go down?'

'Was simple. In my residence in Oxford, they came in one night, and we set up the cards at the table. I cut the cards, but they were already set up by Surly and me. We replaced the deck after each hand. The idea was we were to check the deck in case somebody had fiddled with them. A new deck kept coming in. The cards were cut, exactly into the pattern we wanted. We'd practiced it over the course of two weeks with the other five, someone playing Lafferty each time. He had no chance. Eventually, he went bankrupt.'

'That sounds awkward against a card shark.'

'Warren Kilmartin understood cards to a large degree, but more than that, he understood Lafferty. Lafferty could play cards really well, but he also knew that when he saw the chance, he would go for it. Of course, the chances kept coming up, but what should have been a ninety-five per cent chance had already been fixed to be only five per cent. It took a lot of planning. Surly and I earned that money.'

'How did Lafferty take it?' asked Clarissa.

'He told us all right there and then, he was cheated. Swore he would come for us. It seemed like an empty threat for years. The others got their money. Surly and I got ours. Over the next three or four years, those rather intelligent men started making their way in business. They were good. Very good.

'Carlos was smart but also made money, though. Especially

in those early days. Must have set him up. I tried to keep away from them all as much as possible. When you do something like that, you don't want to be tarnished with it the rest of your life. You don't want to be reminded about it. If I'm honest, my money didn't last that long.'

'I understand what you're saying,' said Clarissa. I understand the situation and I get that we have Miles Lafferty, who's been cheated. There're three dead bodies and I've got you hiding away. Surly's dead as well. How did we get to this? This long?'

'I don't know about the other three bodies,' said Filton. I don't even know where they've been killed. The students haven't been near me since those first five years or so. I didn't watch what they'd done all through life. I didn't care. Trust me, I came to Tobermory to settle down and sell my antiques. Yes, I play a little naughty with it. Get the punters to pay over the odds. Most of them haven't got a darn clue what they're looking at.'

'Clearly,' said Clarissa. 'There's more than that to the story.'

'It was maybe six months ago. Miles Lafferty came here.'

'To your shop?'

'Yes, but I didn't see it coming. He didn't just walk in. I have a daughter who lives on the mainland. She picked up a new boyfriend and had been going with him for a month or two. He was slightly older than her but not the age he should have been. Lafferty, I mean. He looked nearly ten years younger. He was handsome and a charmer.'

'He really was,' said Ellie. 'He flirted with me at one point. I actually went out for dinner with him. Had no idea who he was.'

'The name he used was a false one,' said Filton. 'I know because I've checked since. I've tried to trace him. When someone's coming to kill you, you try to find out where they are. I've had a private detective on it. He can't get near him. Before he left the island, he told me he'd be coming back for me. He told me my daughter didn't deserve to see it. But he'd be back soon. That's when I went underground.'

Clarissa walked back to her chair, and sat down, warming her hands by the fire. 'I think you've been lucky, Mr Pritchard,' said Clarissa.' Not because somebody hasn't come and punched your face for selling modern junk as old tat. Your so-called going underground, your hiding, quite frankly, it was rubbish. I've only been here one day, and I've found you. I found you by going to your shop. If somebody's coming to kill you, you really need to get out of the way. Go to a different country. Change your name. Not shack up with your shop manager.'

Ellie looked shocked.

'Yes, I was looking through the window. Saw the two of you. Seriously, love, you could do better than him. Also, if somebody's coming for him, you don't want to be around. I want to know about your daughter,' said Clarissa.

'She's safe,' said Filton. 'The affair didn't last long. Lafferty ditched her about two weeks later. He was just using her to find me. Never threatened her. He never threatened my family. He just threatened me.'

'And he killed Surly,' said Clarissa. 'Surly lived alone. That's probably why he got killed straight away. Maybe you didn't fit into the time frame. Maybe it was because your daughter was with you. Too much of a connection. Lafferty actually being there.'

'He's a player,' said Ellie. 'When he was over, and I haven't told Filton this, but he did come on to me. I try not to think about it.'

'Why was he coming on to you?' said Clarissa. 'What's the point of that?'

'Maybe it would have been his way back in, back over to the island. His way of keeping tabs on Filton.'

'That makes sense,' said Clarissa. 'Were you and Filton already—?'

'We've been together since about three months after I started working in the shop, but we don't say.'

'Why not?'

'Age thing. I could be Filton's daughter,' said Ellie suddenly. She looked rather retrospective about it.

'Quite a bit of attention brought then. Is that what you were worried about?'

Ellie nodded.

'That's not a bad call,' said Clarissa. 'However, staying here was a bad one. On the bright side, I think at the moment, Miles Lafferty is somewhere in the middle of the ocean on a cruise ship. Because that's where he's just killed off three of the party. You're safe at the moment, but I'm going to put some protection around you. Until we know we've got Lafferty, your life's at risk, Mr Pritchard.'

'I think it's probably safer if I disappear,' said Filton.

'You're going to remain here,' said Clarissa. 'If Lafferty gets off that vessel, we're going to put protection on you. We may look to move you at that point. We are going to know where you are. Because we are going to find him.'

Ellie turned round, put her arms around Filton, kissing him on the cheek. 'You'll be okay now,' she said to him. 'The police are on it. This is a detective inspector. She's high up the chain. They'll get this done. You're safe now, Filton. Listen to her.

You're safe.'

'We'll keep you safe from Lafferty,' said Clarissa, standing up and putting her shawl on. She threw it round over her shoulder and turned for the door and stopped. She sprung back towards him.

'However, I'm coming back to go through that shop of yours. I'll do you for fraud. It's Art, man. It's antiques. You don't mess about with the community like that.' Clarissa tore off towards the door. 'Stay here. Don't go anywhere. Found you once, I'll find you again. Only next time, I'll be angry and mad. You don't want to see that.'

She closed the front door with a bang and walked towards her little green car. She took out her phone. *I wonder what time it is with Macleod*, she said to herself. *Stuff it, Seoras. You put me out here, so you can take a phone call whatever the time of day.*

Chapter 19

Macleod sat in the communications room of the cruise ship, staring at the computer screen in front of him. A woman in a white shirt had come in and set the communications up for him before stepping out, saying that everything should be fine. Macleod looked at the sectional screen in front of him.

In the top right-hand corner, he could see himself. Then on the left was Hope, Clarissa below her, and Ross on the other side. The round robin call had been instigated by Clarissa, as she seemed to have pulled out the original story that had led to the killings. Jane sat behind Macleod, just out of the picture, seemingly half embarrassed to be on the screen. Macleod hated looking at himself and was quietly ignoring the small section where his own face looked back at him.

'How's the cruise?' asked Clarissa. 'Just not entertaining enough for you. I'm sure Jane is pissed.'

'Jane is sitting behind me,' said Macleod. 'And she is not, as you refer to it, pissed.'

'Yes, she is,' said Jane from behind him.

Macleod lifted his eyebrows. 'But before this turns into a free for all,' he said, 'Remember, I need to get moving on this.

I need the story and I need to know what's going on.'

'All right,' said Clarissa. 'Ross and I are still up after night driving. We're not all swanning it around with big restaurants and sun loungers.'

'Some of us haven't even gone out of the office,' said Hope.

'Where's Cunningham?' asked Macleod.

'Susan's off doing a minor task for me. I've got a routine case to look at but I don't think it's a murder. She's taken that to allow me to help you out with this.'

Macleod nodded. 'Clarissa, you start. After all, you seem to have got the jump on what's going on.'

'Right,' said Clarissa. 'Dead Rubber Society, group of people down in Oxford, partly run by an Oxford don who dies. He leaves behind a fortune to be given out to a group of six men, except only five of them get the money. Was his way of teaching them business. Sometimes you have to play dirty to get ahead, something like that.

'John Surly and Filton Pritchard were going to administer the money, make sure that it was taken by those who had actually won it. The idea was they would play cards, only five of them taking away the money. As soon as someone lost his stake, he was out with nothing. The rest of them would take the money that they'd earned at that point.

'Problem was one man, a Miles Lafferty, was a card shark more than capable of playing. Instigated by Warren Kilmartin, the rest got together and bought off Surly and Filton Pritchard so that the game would be rigged. Apparently, according to Filton, it took a while to come up with how they would do it, but they managed it, and Lafferty knew it. He couldn't have been that unlucky that many times.

'Lafferty ended up with nothing. The rest walked away with

a stack of money, including Surly and Filton. They got several thousand for helping out and everybody disappeared off into the rest of their lives. Lafferty was annoyed. However, nothing came of it. We're nearly twenty years back, if not more,' said Clarissa.

'Surly lived alone,' said Ross. 'Don't believe he's spoken to anyone outside of Filton. Someone came to his house, killed him and left his body in the river at the back.'

'Let's hold up a minute,' said Macleod. 'Filton Pritchard still alive, John Surly dead, but dead in Oxford and hidden away in the river. Three people on the cruise, Warren Kilmartin, Professor Carlos Flores, and David Durston, all killed here on the ship. Possibly brought together on the ship. Though we're not sure how. The other two people?'

'Reisenberger and Verde. Fergus Verde, Johann Reisenberger,' said Clarissa, 'Named by Filton Pritchard. At least that's what they were called back then. We need to do a search and find them now.'

'On it,' said Ross and Macleod could hear him already tapping away on his keyboard. *How did he get to work on a screen when the screen was being used for this video?* He never really understood how far Ross could arrange things with technology. He liked one thing happening. Four images were bad enough, four distinct faces looking back at them. One of them his own.

'If I may,' said Jane from behind.

Macleod shifted the chair over. 'Come and sit in the picture.'

'I don't like to, Seoras. I'm not really part of the force.'

'You're one of us,' said Hope. 'What is it? What are you thinking?'

'Here,' said Jane, 'we've had three men die. But the women

involved with them, two wives and a daughter, their faces when you looked at them, when they talked about things, were hiding something. They were out of the cabins when it happened, or they weren't around in the sauna in Flores's case.'

'Just to confirm,' said Macleod. 'Warren Kilmartin was killed in his cabin. Wife was out. Daughter was not around Professor Flores who was killed in the sauna. David Durston killed while his wife was also out.'

'More than that,' said Jane, causing Macleod to raise his eyebrows. 'Women when they were out, one was at the gym, the other was out for a swim. We saw the first woman later on just before they told her. Before that, I think these women were meeting people.'

'Why?' asked Macleod.

'When we talked to them, they had the eyes.'

'The eyes?' queried Macleod.

'They had the eyes,' said Jane. 'When you've been elsewhere, the eyes where you're embarrassed but you're covering it up. They also were at the gym, at the pool. A lot of activity going on around the gym and the pool.'

'Gym and the pool's a good place to go, especially if you're entangled with someone,' said Hope.

'It used to be,' said Clarissa.

'What are we talking about here?' asked Macleod. 'Ross, are you with this?'

Ross was still typing. 'They're saying that the women were meeting someone. I suspect you want to look your best. Some women like to do that in a swimsuit. Some like to be working out. You feel good? You look good.'

'How does he get that, Seoras, and you don't?' asked Clarissa.

'Because Seoras doesn't look at a woman like that,' blurted

167

Jane. 'Well, he does with me.'

There was almost a snigger coming out of Clarissa.

'Seoras would never think of engaging in that sort of activity, taking a woman away from her husband to talk to her somewhere where you could be in public but still acting in a more sexualized fashion.'

'Pulling him in with your looks,' said Clarissa.

'What are you saying?' asked Hope. 'Are you telling us that our killer has pulled these guys in by using the women around them?'

'They're all on the same cruise, aren't they?' said Jane.

'Filton Pritchard has been seen by Lafferty,' said Clarissa. 'If that's who's doing the killings.'

'How come he's not dead?' asked Macleod.

'Because, Seoras, he got hold of Pritchard's daughter—he actually became romantically involved with her; came over on a visit. That's how he found out where Pritchard was. He didn't kill Pritchard then because he'd been connected. Lafferty then breaks up with her. He just hasn't been back yet. If he has, he hasn't found him because Pritchard went undercover. It's a pretty loose cover. I found him inside of the day. I think this is how he's doing it. Jane's got a point.'

Macleod saw the smile on Jane's face.

'If that's the case then, are we saying that the next two are going to be on the boat?' asked Macleod.

'We can check and see,' said Hope.

'Hang on a minute,' said Ross. 'Fergus Verde, he made his money in cars, but according to what I've got here, he's dead. Johann Reisenberger. He's also believed to be dead. A New Age art house start-up went belly up. Disappeared after that.'

'Are they definitely confirmed dead?' asked Macleod.

'Fergus Verde's is dead, pretty definite. Just checked up and we've got a death certificate. Reisenberger is different. Technically, he's missing. Didn't arrive back after so many years. Therefore, dead. It's still a presumed dead.'

'What about Verde's money?' asked Macleod. 'Is our killer still getting the money back? Is the money what upsets him? He doesn't seem to have gone after anyone regarding the family.'

'I can't see Fergus Verde's money,' said Ross. 'I'll have a look and see what we can do. At the moment I can't trace much. Mrs Verde doesn't seem to be that active whereas Fergus Verde was quite easy to get through his financial activity, the commercial aspect.'

'Reisenberger?' asked Macleod.

'That's going to be a fun one, as far as I can see. Art house project though,' said Ross. 'A man missing in the art world. I think we know who to go to for that. She's one for one so far!'

'Are you telling me,' said Clarissa, 'I've got to phone my Frank and tell him I'm on my way again? I got married for a reason, Seoras. You realise that? Jane might be happy to go on the world murder tour with you, but I don't get that privilege. Frank has his golf course to look after.'

'Sorry,' said Macleod. 'We need you to go on this one. Whereabouts was the art house?'

'Edinburgh,' said Ross.

'Fergus Verde?

'All over. He did really well for himself.'

'That's settled then,' said Macleod. 'Ross, you're on the ball for that one. Fergus Verde's yours. Find out if he's got a wife, find out where she is, what's going on. They're probably safe, but hey, we best check it out. Reisenberger is a different issue.

Clarissa, you're on that. Get over to Edinburgh soon as.'

'I can be there tomorrow,' she said. 'I think the ferry's gone tonight.'

'Quick as you can. Get me where he is, what's going on. I haven't got long left on the boat before we dock. I need to know if I'm stopping every passenger coming off. Hope, see if you can find out about Miles Lafferty, what he looks like, anything about him. He obviously hasn't booked under the name of Miles Lafferty. Not coming up on the ship's manifest. If you were coming to kill people, of course you wouldn't. It would be silly. He seems capable of getting passports, capable of finding these other people. Who is he? What did he do? Why did he do it? Who am I up against?'

'Okay, Seoras, will do. Do you need any other assistance when you're landing at port or that?'

'Let the Captain organise that,' said Macleod. 'We might not be going into a British port, so best that he does it all formally that way. I'll back him up if needs be from here.'

'I'm going to get some police to look in on Filton Pritchard,' said Clarissa. 'If that boat docks, Seoras, you need to let me know. We need to get Pritchard safe.'

'Yes, wise precaution,' said Macleod. 'Good idea. To recap, Ross, you're on Verde. Find out who he was. Find out family, wife. Where's the money now? Are they at risk? Clarissa, Reisenberger, where did he go after he was presumed to have died? How difficult would it be to have traced him? If he's still alive, where is he? Hope, Miles Lafferty, that's your domain. Who is he? What did he do with his life? How is he able to get passports, masquerade as other people? How is he a charmer? Why are the women all attracted to him?'

'Will do,' said Hope. 'What are you going to do, Seoras?'

'I'm stuck here at the moment. I need answers from you. If I can get a description of Lafferty, I can look for him. If you can tell me who these other people are, or who their extended family is, I can see if they're on the boat. Until then, I'm hamstrung.'

'That's a pity,' said Clarissa. 'Stuck on a cruise ship, nothing to do. You must be struggling. It must be hell for you. I'm fortunate. I've got all the excitement of Tobermory tonight and an early ferry before racing across to Edinburgh. Isn't it just wonderful? I bet you could wish to be me.'

Macleod frowned at Clarissa's face. 'Look, everyone. Thank you for this. I didn't ask for this. This is our holiday. I may have up to two people who may not yet be dead. We've also Pritchard to protect. Let's get on it. Let's get it done.'

'Of course,' said Ross. 'I'll close the call in a second.'

'Before you do,' said Macleod, 'just to let you all know, if you need me, I'll be in the jacuzzi.'

Jane burst out laughing behind Macleod. He didn't always have a great sense of humour, but Clarissa had annoyed him with the comment. He'd had his holiday ruined. His partner was now working alongside him, and albeit she contributed brilliantly, he'd rather have been enjoying dinner with her. Tremendous views, sightseeing, enjoying a spa with her. Instead, he was on the investigation trudge, piling around a ship, desperately looking for a murderer.

Clarissa didn't get to tease like that.

'Don't get too poached,' said Clarissa. 'I can close my own call down, Ross. Just sort the boss's out.'

Macleod sat back in the chair as one by one the screens disappeared, Hope gave a little hand wave and said goodbye to Jane before hers closed. Macleod turned to Jane. 'You did well,' he said. 'That's a superb line of attack, a fantastic thought.'

'Tell me something, is it always like this? I always thought you guys would be deadly serious. There'd be lots of thinking like you do when you're on your own.'

'Why do you think I get away on my own?' said Macleod. 'How do you seriously think with that lot about?' Jane watched his impassable face for a moment, and then Macleod broke into a smile. 'They tell me I can't do humour,' he said. 'Maybe it's you that brings it out in me.'

'We've got a jacuzzi to get into,' she said. 'Come on.'

He stood up. She gave him a little smack on the bottom. 'That was a joke,' he said. 'I'm on a case. I can't be seen in a jacuzzi.'

'You think I don't know that,' she said. 'I, however, am only on a temporary assignment. I can go wherever I want.' She leaned forward and kissed him. 'It's been good,' she said. 'I'm seeing a little of you at work. I'm seeing more of you than I've ever seen from that side of it.'

He smiled and put his hand out. As she took his hand, she grinned at him. 'I'm not put off,' she said. 'You're not the same Seoras at work, but I still like him.'

Chapter 20

C larissa Urquhart drove her green sports car along the Edinburgh ring road. She had set off early that morning, catching the ferry from Mull across to Oban, before racing as fast as she could towards Glasgow. From there, she took the motorway over to Edinburgh.

She'd only stopped for a couple of minutes. A quick toilet run, and more coffee. She was tired. At her age, she was fed up with this racing about. That was the problem with the murder team. They were always worried that somebody else was going to get killed. Art was so much more relaxed. You didn't worry about things like that. Sure, priceless items may have got stolen, but there was more decorum, more flair to it.

Reisenberger's art house project had taken place on the edge of Edinburgh. According to details Ross had sent her through, he had bought a large building on the edge of a new estate some twenty years ago. The estate was now run down, but the building was still there, even though he didn't own it.

As she came off the Edinburgh ring road driving in towards the estate, Clarissa could see that difference which happened so starkly in cities. You passed a rather posh area, and everything looked good. Houses were neatly done. Suddenly, she was driving onto an estate and saw an upturned shopping trolley. There were people hanging about looking like they didn't know what to do. That never happened in the posher areas. They'd have been moved on.

Clarissa wasn't bothered, though. She was here to find out a story, not to solve the social problems of an estate. She pulled up in front of the art house building, looked up and saw it was now a youth club retreat. A banner that had seen slightly better days hung over a doorway. Stepping out of the little green car, she flung her shawl over her shoulder and reluctantly marched up to a door that she found to be open. It creaked as she entered a hallway with a tiled floor. It felt cold inside.

'Can I help you?' shouted a voice. A woman of equivalent age faced Clarissa from the far end of the hall. She had a mop in her hand.

'Hi,' said Clarissa. 'I'm sorry to bother you.' She reached inside her shawl to pull out her warrant card. 'Detective Inspector Clarissa Urquhart. I'm actually looking for some information.'

The woman stepped fully out from the doorway she was standing in. 'I will help you as best I can,' she said. 'What are you looking for?'

'Information about Reisenberger, Johan Reisenberger. I believe this building was once his.'

'Blimey, that's a long time ago,' the woman said.

Clarissa walked up the hallway, her boots clipping loudly across the floor. 'Is there anywhere else we could sit?'

'Yes, it's not very warm, is it? We try to go easy on the heating. It's the cost.'

'Oh, well, if that's a problem,' said Clarissa. 'Or actually, is there anywhere we could sit over a coffee? A café, perhaps?

Do you know a lot about Reisenberger?'

'I was here at the time,' said the woman. 'My name's Andrea, Andrea Macleod.'

They're flipping everywhere, thought Clarissa. *Bad enough when you go up to the northwest.*

'I tell you what. There's a cafe just around the corner. We could go there. That's usually warm.'

'Brilliant,' said Clarissa.

'Give me five minutes. I want to finish this bit of the floor and I'll need to lock up. Can't leave a building like this open with nobody in it.'

'I'm outside in the little green sports car. Come and join me, and then we'll pop round the corner.'

Andrea Macleod stepped into Clarissa's car ten minutes later and they drove less than a quarter of a mile. The cafe was cheery looking enough, but inside, it was all white mugs and saucers. Clarissa was actually surprised when she saw a coffee machine. It had an automatic system. She thought little of the coffee that would come out of it, but she needed something to keep her awake. Andrea took a cup of tea. Clarissa brought the drinks back in the white mugs and sat down, placing a cream bun in front of each of them. She'd had little for breakfast.

'Andrea, tell me, Johan Reisenberger, what happened with him? Is he actually dead?'

'Oh, he's dead all right,' said Andrea. 'He died with no children and no wife. The art house project was excellent, but Johan liked a bit of the old drugs. Liked to get high. Said it worked brilliantly for his creative side. He'd come up here with a lot of money, as far as I could make out. I was employed at the time to do the cleaning in the place. I've always cleaned that place. Can't seem to get away from here.'

Clarissa looked over at the woman. She had the face every one of Clarissa's age had. There were the lines, except they seemed to be more so on this woman. Life didn't seem to have treated her as well as Clarissa. The woman certainly didn't have a panache about her, although she was a pleasant enough person.

'So, what, the building just became yours?'

'The thing was, Helen Carlisle was around back in those days. Helen Carlisle was a good friend of Johan's.'

'When you say good friend, how good? Like partner? Like lover?'

'Oh, lover. The two of them were into some quite weird sex. It was like hippie time, only the noughties. Hippies from when they shouldn't have been hippies. He almost was a blast from the past, not that I remember that time that well myself. I was a '70s child.'

'Did Johan blow his fortune?' asked Clarissa.

'Oh, no, there was money left over. In fact, it was given to Helen.'

'She didn't think of keeping the place going?'

'She looked at it for a while, but Johan, he never really had a proper idea. He had this money, and he had the idea of forming a commune. To be honest, I think from what I knew of him, and I wasn't close to him, he seemed more in love with the idea of the sex and the whole wild lifestyle around it. He didn't really seem to create that much art. Projects just fell apart. She was certainly wiser without him. She was stoned half the time when he was here. That was the thing. You see, Helen disappeared.'

Clarissa looked down at her coffee, took a sip of it, found out it was warm but more like a milky coffee, not the latte she'd ordered. People who don't know coffee shouldn't make it and these machines were certainly rubbish at it. Macleod always insisted on well-done coffee and Clarissa thought she had spoiled herself. Not that she disagreed with him. Seoras and she were different, very different people, but with coffee, they had similar exacting standards. Thankfully, Ross had been up to them.

'Would you have any idea where Helen Carlisle is?'

'She disappeared. I mean, never seen her back around this place. The thing was, at the time, it was strange.'

'In what way was it strange?' asked Clarissa.

'Well,' said Andrea, 'there was a whole rumour about an Orthodox church. There are more Orthodox churches now, but the one at the time no longer exists. There was a Latvian statue within it. I knew nothing about it, but apparently, it was worth a bit. I don't know the backstory, but I remember them saying that the Latvian statue was worth a bit, and it went missing.

'Well, we found out that the orthodox priest came round and accused Helen Carlisle. Said she had stolen it. Helen denied all knowledge of that, but Helen disappears about two months later, sells the building, never comes back. The priest was adamant for the four or five years afterwards. The church then sold their building. They moved. He was sent back to Latvia. It was a bit strange, all in all. He was deeply interested in it, though, deeply offended when it was taken. They couldn't trace it, though. Police were involved. To be honest, I don't think they were that bothered. Art is not really a big thing with the police, is it?'

Clarissa looked up suddenly. 'Actually, I'm part of the Inverness art team.'

'So, you are seeking the statue? Is the statue what you're interested in?'

'No, it's not. That's not what I'm about. I'm just trying to trace Johan Reisenberger and what happened to him and the surrounding people, so you've been very helpful.'

'Well, to be honest, I had to think about it about eighteen months ago. In fact, I had to do a bit of research. There was a man that came around asking all about Johan. He seemed a little perturbed that he was dead.'

'Who? What did he look like?'

'Oh, blimey. He wore like one of those hats. I don't know what they call them. Indiana Jones wore them, something like that, but he didn't look like Harrison Ford. In fact, he was well made up. I thought I don't see many men wearing that amount of makeup. It's strange. I'm not sure it was his actual face. Quite fat in the cheeks, but in a good way. To be honest, he was one of those younger guys you thought if you could get away with it, you'd certainly have a good time with him.'

Clarissa wasn't that sure she knew and now wondered if Frank was taming her a little.

'Did the man leave a name?'

'He said he was Steven. Didn't give me a second name. He took me out for dinner at one point because he'd asked me to go away and find a lot of this information out. I talked to different people, but I couldn't go any further with it. But I got a dinner out of him, which was nice. A rather nice place, too.'

'When you talked to him, what was he concerned about?'

'He wanted to trace Johan like you. He wanted to know where Johan was. "Johan's six feet under the ground," I told him.'

'When you told him that, how did he react?' asked Clarissa.

'Disappointed, but then he asked about the money. I'm sure he was trying to trace where the money was going.'

'How did he seem?'

'Well, he was pretty even about it. He said he was writing a book at one point. The thing was, when I told him that the building had been sold, and the palaver about the Latvian statue, and Helen Carlisle, he got really quite agitated then. He seemed angry. He said nothing to me, but you could tell he was fuming.'

'What did he ask you about Helen Carlisle?' prompted Clarissa.

'Well, he pushed for that. Wanted to know where she'd gone. Wanted to know everything about her. There's not a lot to find out. In the end, he thanked me. He paid for dinner and made a donation to what we do here at the club. I mean, he was generally quite a decent person.'

Clarissa nodded. She finished her cup of coffee and ate her cream bun, letting Andrea eat up too. She then took the woman back in the car to the building. As Andrea was getting out, she stopped and looked back into the car at Clarissa.

'You asked about his mood and stuff. It was very intense; I can tell you that. Very, very intense. I remember I got a wee bit agitated at one point because he seemed so forceful asking a question. The one thing about him was he switched like that.'

'In what way?' asked Clarissa.

'He made you feel good. He was incredible at pushing your buttons. Now, I'm not saying I felt sexually attracted to him. It wasn't like we were going to run off and disappear behind a bike shed somewhere,' laughed Andrea, 'but he could play you, you know. He could sense the way you were and react to it. To be honest, it was brilliant. It was lovely. I enjoyed that thoroughly. He made you feel good. He made you feel special. I could see him being a charmer. I could see him winding the ladies around his little finger.'

Clarissa had the feeling she'd heard about this man before.

'I might send a sketch artist your way,' said Clarissa. 'Get him to draw up a lifelike image of the person you met or we might ask you to the station. They do it in different ways now. I'm no expert on it.'

'Oh, I'm happy enough to do that,' she said. 'Don't suppose I'll get another cup of tea and a cream bun, do you?'

Clarissa laughed. 'If that's what it takes, that's what I'll buy you, but it won't be me. I've got to get on and find that Latvian statue.'

'Are you seriously from like, an art squad?' said Andrea.

'Yes,' said Clarissa.

'That's a long time chasing up a theft like that, though, isn't it?'

'I'm not chasing the theft,' started Clarissa, but then she stopped and just smiled. 'Yes, it is.'

She watched the woman disappear back into the hall. *Imagine spending your life in one place*, thought Clarissa. *One place like this, seeing all the comings and goings. It's a different sort of art.*

Clarissa spent her time seeing things from all around the world, looking at how they told the history of people, places, civilisations. This woman saw the history of a place by living through it. She was a living relic herself. That should have sounded better.

Clarissa started up the car and drove off. She needed to sit down somewhere with her laptop and investigate this Latvian statue. Maybe she could get old stories about it. Then she thought about what she just said. If anybody had called her a relic or thought she was one, she'd have put the boot into them. *Something to remember, though*, she thought. *History is in the people; it's not always in the things.* She smiled as she drove off to find another cafe to sit with her laptop. It was time to go digging, just not with a trowel.

Chapter 21

Ross had popped in to speak with the Oxfordshire police, assisting with their own inquiries about what had happened at Surly's house. As soon as he was clear from that, he set up at a desk within the station to look further into Fergus Verde.

Fergus Verde had done well as a car salesman. He'd opened multiple forecourts across the country. Although his name was never at the forefront of these apparently independent forecourts, he was certainly the brains and the money behind them.

His fortune had grown until his untimely death. It had been a skiing accident out on the pistes of Italy and Ross had phoned the Italian police to check the incident. The man had certainly been certified dead, and the body had been repatriated to Britain. His wife, however, had married a travel critic, a man called Ottomeyer, and the fortune now resided with them both. Ross wondered what it meant. Would somebody like Miles Lafferty be prepared to chase and to go after them? He called up Hope to see if she had come up with anything on Miles Lafferty.

'Alan,' she said, 'yes, I've been digging into it. I've sent some people around to where Lafferty used to live in the Oxfordshire area. They got me a few snapshots. Apparently, he was a highly driven guy, angry when he lost. They got me an old girlfriend who put me in touch with one of her friends who dated him later in life. They said that Lafferty always carried a grudge about money and about certain people who seemed to have a lot more of it than he had. Constantly told her he didn't get the start that he should have had—that he was cheated out of it.'

'That sounds promising,' said Ross. 'Did they know where he is now?'

'He'd gone off the radar about five years ago. I can't find anybody who knows him. Tried looking for a last known address and Miles Lafferty doesn't seem to exist now. He's not anywhere.'

'That's quite something,' said Ross, 'to make yourself disappear.'

'Up to five years ago,' said Hope, 'there was someone there. His house in Oxfordshire was sold and moved on, and his bank account was closed. Everything about him was closed down, and suddenly he wasn't there anymore. What I found out was that he had been taking theatrical classes and had done a makeup course. Apparently, he was also struggling at times to make ends meet, so he'd gone off to get a job on the oceans.'

'If he went and worked on the cruise ships, he'd have time away to do what he needed to do and then earn his money,' said Ross. 'He wouldn't be tied to one place for a lot of the time. He'd be able to drive his agendas in between sailings.'

'Exactly. He's fitting the bill,' said Hope. 'He also was a climber. But we don't know who he is anymore. We don't know where he is.'

'That's fine, except I don't understand where he's getting connections for passports in that.'

'Oh, that's easy,' said Hope. 'He was a card shark, and he worked for some rather nasty people for a while, playing cards with them, assisting them. It wouldn't be that hard to find out from them how to do passports, et cetera.'

'Have we got a description of what he looks like?'

'Average height, average build. Wouldn't notice him in a crowd,' said Hope. 'I've had a few people try to describe him to me, but there's not a lot noticeable about him. Not a lot that draws you to him. Eye colour seems to have changed over time, too.'

'Contacts, then,' said Ross. 'Amazing that he attracts the women though. That's not good. Phone Macleod and tell the boss what I've told you. I'm going to see if I can find Ottomeyer.'

'Will do, Alan? If you find him, give us a ring.'

Ross put the phone down and went to make a cup of coffee, sitting back down at his makeshift desk. He looked up the offices of the publications Ottomeyer wrote for as a travel critic. On contacting a few of them, he found out that he didn't work directly from there. Instead, he worked from home. Fortunately, once Ross advised he was a police officer in desperate need to contact Ottomeyer, he was given a number for his house.

Ross sat listening to the phone ringing, wondering if anyone would pick up. At first, it went to an answering machine, and Ross hung up. He called back. It rang through to the answering machine again. When it asked him to leave a message, this time Ross left his mobile number, saying that if anyone was there, they needed to contact him directly and quickly.

Ross put the phone down and stood up to stretch his back, tired from the driving he'd done recently. As he did so, his phone vibrated in his pocket. It was an unknown number, and he answered. 'This is Detective Constable Alan Ross. Who's speaking?'

'This is Maria,' said a voice from the other end. It certainly wasn't a British voice.

'Hello, Maria,' said Ross. 'How can I help?'

'You have just phoned Mr Ottomeyer's phone. I am his cleaner, so I ring you back.'

'Brilliant,' said Ross. 'I'm trying to get a hold of Mr Ottomeyer. Do you know where he is?'

'Yes, he's away.'

'Away where?' asked Ross.

'Away with his wife, Tara. Said he went on a cruise. I have the magazines here.'

'When did they go?' asked Ross, 'and when are they back?'

'Not due back for two weeks. Went over a week ago. Tara insisted he go on the cruise. He wasn't keen, but she said to go. She'd been funny.'

'What do you mean funny?' asked Ross.

'Going out. She went out different times, away from Mr Ottomeyer. They usually went together, but recently she went on her own too. I don't interfere,' said Maria.

'Did she dress up at all to do these things?'

'Always dressed up. I think she told someone, though. I overheard her once with friends saying about some man, young man, she liked a lot, but I don't interfere. Just a housekeeper. I need this job, so you keep quiet, yes?'

'Yes,' said Ross. 'If I can, I just need to find them. Do you know what cruise ship they're on?'

'No, I didn't involve the booking, but I have found magazine. It's Lineways, yes? Lineways. They book through Lineways.'

'Thank you,' said Ross. 'But I'm not sure who Lineways is.'

'I have number.' Maria passed a number to Ross, who thanked her before closing the call. He made a note of the phone number Maria was ringing from because it wasn't the same as Ottomeyer's. Possibly her own mobile. He then contacted the number she'd given him.

'Lineway's Travel Agents.'

'Hello, it's Detective Constable Alan Ross. I need to find out about a booking you may have made for a Mr Ottomeyer.'

'Yes, we do lots of bookings for Mr Ottomeyer. He's a travel critic. Did you know that?'

'Yes,' said Ross, 'I know that. I just need to know where he is now. What cruise ship?'

'Hang on a moment,' the woman said. He could hear her punching in some numbers, and then she passed over the cruise line they were on and details of the ship. Ross's heart thumped. *That's it. That's the one Macleod's on,* he thought.

He closed down the call quickly and then rang the vessel directly.

'Yes, you're speaking to the first officer,' said a voice.

'Hello, this is Detective Constable Alan Ross working with Detective Chief Inspector Macleod. I need you to get a message to him. Take this down, please. Ottomeyer is on board the vessel. He married the wife of Fergus Verde, who's dead. Tara, his wife, has gone with Ottomeyer on a cruise. Believes she may have been having an affair with a younger man before she went. Believes she's in trouble.'

'I'll get that to him directly, sir,' said the first officer. Ross put the phone down. He hoped he was in time because it looked like Ottomeyer or possibly Tara were in trouble.

Scene break, scene break, scene break.

Macleod heard the doorbell ring on his cabin door and stood up from the sofa. He'd been dozing for five minutes, catching a bit of sleep when he could.

'Who's that?' asked Jane from upstairs.

'I haven't even got there yet,' said Macleod. He looked through the peephole to see one of the crew standing before the door. Macleod opened it and the crewman was holding an envelope which he handed to Macleod. Macleod brought it inside, opened it up and read the words on the paper.

'Jane,' he shouted as he got towards the end.

'What's up, Seoras?'

'Fergus Verde's dead, but his wife seems to have been having an affair. She's here with her new husband, a Mr Ottomeyer. We need to find them.'

Macleod raced to the door, calling back the crew member. He was now halfway down the corridor. The young man turned and ran back.

'Listen, get upstairs to the Captain. Tell the Captain we need to find Ottomeyer. What cabin he's in. Go, go!'

As the junior crew member ran off, Jane marched to the door of the cabin behind Macleod. 'Where are we going?'

'We need to go quickly. I've just sent him off for information. Come on, we're heading up towards the bridge.'

Together they strode along, finally getting into a lift and making their way up to the bridge. As they arrived on the top deck racing to the bridge, the Captain came out of his ready room towards Macleod.

'Should have stayed where you were. He's in a cabin round the corner from you.'

'Blimey,' said Macleod. Jane had already turned, and they started running back. The Captain followed, hot on their heels. It took them only a couple of minutes to get there. On approaching the door, Macleod rang the bell. Before anyone could answer, he was thumping already on the door. It opened a few seconds later with a rather annoyed-looking man there.

'What is wrong?' It was a German accent, or maybe Austrian, somewhere over that part of Europe, Macleod thought.

'Is your name, Ottomeyer?'

'Yes, I'm Ottomeyer. I'm a travel critic. What is the meaning of this?' He looked beyond Macleod. 'Captain, what are you doing? What is this?'

'I'm Detective Chief Inspector Seoras Macleod. I'm investigating murders on this vessel, and I believe you may be in danger. Is your wife in there with you? '

'No, she's gone up to the promenade deck. She went for a walk. In fact, she should be back here by now. I don't know what's keeping her.'

Macleod didn't finish the conversation. He just turned and ran, desperately reaching the nearest elevator. As he waited for the doors to open, Jane caught up with him, the Captain following behind.

'We've got to get up there. We've got to find her.'

'Shouldn't we get a description?' asked Jane.

'Time is of the essence,' said Macleod. 'Captain, go bring him. Bring him back up with us.'

Macleod jumped into the lift. As it got up to the promenade deck, he stepped out and opened a large door to outside air. He strode around the outside of the vessel.

'Mrs Ottomeyer. Tara. Tara Ottomeyer. I'm looking for Tara Ottomeyer.'

Macleod walked all the way around the promenade, which took him nearly five minutes. The vessel was enormous, and Jane walked the opposite direction until they met back on the other side.

'Nothing. Nothing.'

They continued on their way round. As Macleod came round for a second time, he saw Jane talking to someone. He ran over.

'Seoras, this is Marjorie. Marjorie was talking to Tara Ottomeyer.'

'When?' asked Macleod.

'Fifteen minutes ago. She was over there with a young man when I left her.'

'What was it like on deck? Were there many people about?'

'Quite quiet.'

Macleod looked over to where the woman had showed Tara Ottomeyer had been. He strode over, seeing the Captain approaching from the far side. As he stopped at the indicated point, he looked over the railings, down to the sea below. He was at the aft of the vessel. He looked up, but the deck above planed out above him, making a small roof. Someone above could not see down to where he was, but below him, there were no cabin windows.

He saw Mr Ottomeyer behind the Captain. 'Jane,' he said to her, 'Go beyond the Captain. Take Mr Ottomeyer, ask him anything. Just keep him away from me for a minute.' Jane tore off as the Captain arrived.

'Captain,' said Macleod, 'if I threw somebody off here, would anybody on the ship see them?'

189

The Captain stopped for a moment, thinking, looking left and right. 'No,' he said. 'I would doubt it.'

'I believe you have someone overboard. Last fifteen minutes.'

'How?'

'She was here. Tara Ottomeyer was here with someone, a young man, and then the deck was empty. I believe she's gone overboard. We've searched. We can't find her.'

'She could have just gone below. She could be anywhere on the ship,' said the Captain.

'Turn,' said Macleod, 'do what you do. You must know how to look for somebody overboard.'

'Of course,' said the Captain, 'but who's to say she really is? She could be anywhere.'

'Do it now,' said Macleod. 'It's my honest belief she's gone over. We can search the rest of the ship. We can put a call out for her but start your search. How long can someone last in these waters?'

The Captain looked at him. 'Depends on a lot of things. Method of entry, for one. Was she conscious hitting the water? It's a heck of a fall too from here. Excuse me, I'll get things underway.'

He tore off to a nearby phone and Macleod looked out of the aft of the vessel. He knew that Mr Ottomeyer was now approaching him.

The vessel turned slowly around.

'What's happening?' asked Ottomeyer, suddenly panicked. 'What's happening?'

'I believe your wife may have gone overboard, sir,' said Macleod. 'We're going to search for her.'

Macleod watched as the man almost broke down in front of him. He collapsed to his knees.

'Jane,' shouted Macleod, 'go find a first aider, paramedic, someone. Get the doctor for this man.'

We're too late, thought Macleod. In his bones, he felt it. They were too late.

Chapter 22

Clarissa sat in front of her laptop, searching for details in the newspapers of the past about the Latvian statue, stolen from an church in Edinburgh. It wasn't easy to do. She looked under several terms, including the Orthodox Church, eventually finding a record for it on an out-of-date Orthodox Church website.

Clarissa got the name of the statue, the type it was, and realised that it was actually a valuable asset, probably worth nearly fifteen thousand pounds nowadays. She thought about how it would be moved on. It wasn't special enough not to appear, certainly after several years, in auction houses. Not a one-off. It wasn't singular. There had been several of them made, and she wondered if any had come up for sale. Clarissa looked through the auction houses who could handle that sort of material. She trawled down through records, past sales, eventually finding one at an auction house in Somerset. She looked at the phone number and rang it, calling up the front office of the auction house.

'Hello?' said a voice.

'Hello. This is Detective Inspector Clarissa Urquhart. I wonder if you could help me.'

'How can I help you, Detective Inspector?'

Clarissa detailed the statue, and what she thought was the selling date at that auction house, and asked if she could be sent the purchase record. The woman hesitated for a moment, but then delved into her records, asking Clarissa to wait. Two minutes later, the woman read the purchase record to Clarissa, who was surprised to see that the seller had a Scottish Borders address.

'Pass me that again,' said Clarissa, taking out a pen. She wrote the address, just outside Selkirk. She thanked the woman before closing down her laptop, and putting her stuff in her bag. Going onto her maps function on the phone, she plotted a route straight there.

Feeling rather drained, Clarissa was perked up. This could be it. The green car hammered out of Edinburgh, taking the road south. As she sped along the single carriageway, Clarissa drove past other cars, foot to the floor, swinging in and out of the traffic.

She could see the odd annoyed look from other drivers, but she was safe. Well, safe enough. Hammering along, she arrived in Selkirk, stopping at a house near the edge of the town. She turned the car straight up the driveway, jumped out, and threw her shawl around her. Clarissa marched up to the front door, where she banged on it loudly, before realising there was a bell to one side.

There was a shout of, 'I'm coming,' and then a couple of minutes later, the door opened. The woman standing there was probably heading into her fifties.

'Excuse me,' said Clarissa, realising she was slightly out of breath. 'My name is Detective Inspector Clarissa Urquhart. I've come about a Latvian statue that was sold at an auction house in Somerset. Your name is on the purchase record for it, saying that you had sold it. It gave this address. Can you just confirm your name for me?'

'It's quite a story, and yes, I did sell that one, and it was down in Somerset. It's not where we were at the time.'

'I don't understand,' said Clarissa. 'Why did you sell it down there?'

'Apparently, it was a good place to sell it. It wasn't sold for me. It was sold for my sister's partner.'

'Who's your sister?'

'My sister is Jenny. Jenny Starry. I'm Angela Starry. Neither of us is married.'

'Who's your sister's partner?' asked Clarissa. She was expecting a man's name, expecting that this was a dead end. When the woman said the name, Clarissa became thoughtful.

'Leila. Leila Massloe.'

'What age is Leila?' asked Clarissa.

'Oh, forties. Early forties, I think.'

Leila Massloe, thought Clarissa. *I've come all this way and Leila Massloe is in her forties. Maybe?*

'You don't know if Leila had a previous name?'

'Well, she was a Helen at one point. I'm not sure what else. She calls herself Leila now.'

'Just Helen. Can you think, please, it's important? Can you remember her surname?'

'Okay. Hang on,' said the woman. 'I remember her name. It was Helen, but it was a town. An English town.'

'Carlisle?' asked Clarissa.

'That's it. Helen Carlisle.'

'Where is your sister?' asked Clarissa suddenly.

'My sister? I'm not sure. Hang on a minute. I'll tell you what.

I'll call her. Come on in.'

Clarissa stepped inside the house, which was well furnished. There were a few family photographs up. As the woman dialled the phone, she turned to Clarissa pointing to the wall.

'That's my sister up there. That's Jenny. Over there, that's Helen with her. Helen's been with her for a while now. Oh, her phone's ringing out. She's not answering. I don't know where she is. Maybe I'll try her mobile.'

'Was Helen quite rich?' asked Clarissa.

'Oh, yes. Jenny's not short of money, but Helen had real money. Could do anything with Helen.'

'What was Helen like?'

'Honestly, I think she's a bit new ageist. Oh, she was always off about the moon and the sun and all that sort of stuff. She was good for Jenny. Jenny and she got on well. They still do. That's funny.'

'What?' asked Clarissa, looking at Angela. The woman was blonde of hair, with a rather petite build, but the worry on her face at the moment was getting to Clarissa.

'There's no response at all. Oh, hang on.'

'Hang on what?' asked Clarissa.

'She was going away. She was going somewhere. Where was she going? Sorry. They do this a lot. Okay. She mentions to me suddenly that she's going away, and it's like for a couple of weeks. She's probably known about it for a few months, maybe more. Then she suddenly announces it.'

'Where was she going? Think!' said Clarissa. 'It's important.'

'She mentioned several places. A number of places, because they were stopping in them. She's cruising,' said the woman. 'She's going cruising.'

'Where?'

195

'I've no idea. I was right though; she was up here and she said to me, she said, "Leila's had an idea, and she got it from a guy she was not long introduced to."'

'In what way?'

'Jenny's quite open about the relationship. Her and Leila, they see other people even though they're very close together. Apparently, there was some younger lad came up. He had taken Leila out and he was suggesting what to do. They were going to go on a cruise. I remember, because it was a particular cruise. He had sold this idea of how this cruise was so good. Said he would be on it as well.'

'You didn't get a name for him, did you?'

'No surname, but he was called Peter. That's all I know. I know nothing else about him. I never got to see him.'

Clarissa took out her phone and walked over to the photographs on the wall. She started taking pictures.

Angela Starry looked over at her. 'You look really worried,' she said. 'Is my sister in danger?'

'I don't know,' said Clarissa. 'Give me a moment.'

She looked up the call list on her phone and dialled over to Macleod's cruise ship. It gave a strange ringing tone before it was picked up.

'This is Detective Inspector Clarissa Urquhart working with Detective Chief Inspector Macleod. I need to speak to him.'

'I'm afraid the inspector's charging around at the moment. We're quite busy.'

'In what way?' asked Clarissa.

'We've had someone go overboard, or so your inspector suspects.'

'You need to get a message to him,' said Clarissa. 'I'm at the house of an Angela Starry. Her sister Jenny Starry may be on board the vessel with a Leila Massloe, M-A-S-S-L-O-E. You need to find them. I believe Leila Massloe is the inheritor of the wealth of Johann Reisenberger. She may be the next victim.'

'I'll convey that to your inspector directly.'

'Who does he think has gone in the water?' asked Clarissa.

'He said a Tara Ottomeyer. She's definitely on the ship.'

'Can you look up the passenger list for me and see if you can find Leila Massloe?'

'I'll start doing that for you now,' said the man.

'Don't come back to me. If you get a cabin number or whatever, get it to Macleod. He needs to know.'

Clarissa closed the call and stood pondering what she'd just heard.

'Is my sister all right?' asked Angela Starry.

'Unknown,' said Clarissa. 'I really don't know. It's hard to get information at the moment. That was the crew of the cruise ship. I didn't get to speak to my inspector. Apparently, someone else has gone in the water, but he doesn't believe it's your sister.'

The woman stared at Clarissa. 'What's going on?' she said.

'Your sister's friend, Leila Massloe, may have inherited money that someone thinks she shouldn't have or at least thinks is theirs. He seems to be on a vendetta to act against these people,' said Clarissa, not wanting to panic the woman anymore.

'Dear goodness,' she said.

'I'll be in touch,' said Clarissa, 'as soon as I can. You could try phoning your sister. Although it doesn't look like the mobile signal's getting through. If you get in contact with her, email, whatever, please just tell her she needs to get to see the Captain immediately along with Leila. Or tell her to find Detective Chief Inspector Macleod.'

The woman nodded and disappeared off, presumably to get to her computer or tablet and write that email.

Clarissa stepped out of the house, walking back to the green car. She didn't get in, but stood at the side of it, feeling the wind blowing across her. It was a sturdy wind. She was now going to have to return to Inverness. Then she wondered if that was the best course of action. Undecided, she placed a call to Hope up in the Inverness station.

'How are we getting on?' Hope asked Clarissa, seeing who it was at the end of the call.

'I've tracked down a Leila Massloe,' said Clarissa, and detailed all the steps she'd taken to Hope.

'That sounds good. Ross also found a Tara Ottomeyer, saying that she had taken the fortune of Fergus Verde.'

'There's nobody else left then,' said Clarissa. 'I think we've covered off all the bases. What do you want me to do?'

'It would be best to stay in the area in case the boss gets back, ask for any more details. Answer any questions, especially your last interviewee, from what you've said.'

'I suppose so,' said Clarissa. 'But what? I just kick my heels?'

'Yes, Ross is going to do the same. Seoras asked for our help. It looks like it's up to him now.'

'From what I've heard, he's already looking for somebody gone overboard.'

There was a sigh on the end of the phone. 'What's up,' asked Clarissa.

'He gets all the fun; do you know that?' said Hope. 'I move up to Detective Inspector, and he's meant to be running the show from above, and all of a sudden, he's off charging around again. Goes on a cruise ship and he gets bodies. I sometimes think the sooner he retires, the sooner the place will be safer.'

Clarissa laughed at the other end of the phone. 'That's why I've headed off to the art world,' she said.

'He's going to miss you in that sense.'

'I'll see him every day. I work in an office near to you, round the corner. You can come and say hello. He'll be saying hello, no doubt. I'll have to explain to him about the art world. Not looking forward to that.'

'He came straight to you though; did you notice that? Didn't send Cunningham out. He still doesn't have his Rottweiler to replace you.'

'I'm in the art world now. You don't get to call me the Rottweiler.'

'Yet, you are. At the end of Macleod's leash,' said Hope.

Clarissa said nothing in return. She'd be back on the arts case soon. It's what she wanted, and what she needed. Certainly not to be away from Frank like this.

'Let me know if you need anything else then,' said Clarissa. 'I'll stay local for tonight, and head back up tomorrow.'

'Get some rest,' said Hope. 'You've been charging around like anything, you and Ross.'

'Working for Macleod, you see; the man doesn't change,' said Clarissa.

She closed the call and gave a sigh, looking around her. There was a decent antique shop in Selkirk, she thought. Maybe she could kill the afternoon there. She climbed inside the little green sports car, satisfied she'd done her work, and drove off.

Chapter 23

Macleod stood on the promenade deck but had moved away from the aft of the ship. He was now wandering along the side, Jane walking with him. The entire operation had been quite something else.

The large vessel had turned around, presumably retracing the track it had come along. Macleod was unsure because all around them was the sea. The Captain had disappeared off to make sure everything was happening, while a member of the crew was attending to Mr Ottomeyer. He was desperately looking over the side.

Macleod had seen several rescue vessels launched from the ship, and they were going back and forward from it. Some type of search pattern, Macleod believed. He'd heard something about a herringbone, but he wasn't sure that was the correct term. If Tara was in the water, it was up to the Captain and his people. Macleod was out of his depth with this one.

He now stood with both hands on the railing of the ship. The killer was obviously clever. Somehow lured her to the aft of the ship before dumping her in. Was this another case of a woman being attracted to him? Macleod found it hard to get his head around how so many women could be lured to him, but he was clearly not being the same man with each one.

How long had it been since she entered the water? Macleod had always heard that you really wanted to get people within the first fifteen to twenty minutes. At that point, they were more likely to be alive. The Captain had said something about the method of entry. He guessed, if she'd fallen all that way from the promenade deck, she could indeed have been dead on hitting the water. Maybe broke her neck. He had said nothing to Mr Ottomeyer. If he couldn't see the grimness of the situation at this point, you wouldn't be convincing him with logic. You'd just have to hold him through it.

'They're still going in and out, Seoras. I don't know how far we are. Have we gone fifteen minutes in the other direction?'

'We'll go more than that, though,' said Macleod. 'You have to consider the drift. I don't know what the sea's doing. I can't tell from up here.'

He looked at his watch. *Fifteen minutes, twenty minutes, twenty-five minutes. What was it?* The vessel turned again. It looked like it was going back on the track it had gone before. Maybe it was different. Maybe it was slightly off to one side.

The only good news was that the vessel would now take longer to get to port. It would give Macleod more of a chance, but he needed Clarissa to come through. Ross had done. Ross had discovered what he needed to. They were just too late.

Unless, of course, Tara Ottomeyer was somewhere on the vessel. He hoped so. He hoped that his assumption she'd been thrown off the aft of the ship was an error, but his heart said he wasn't wrong.

It was a problem Macleod had. Too often, he was too correct. He understood killers. He understood their motivation, when they would act. There was no better spot to throw someone off that vessel than the one the man had chosen. And, of course, if they were being secret about whatever they were doing, it was perfect because no one would be about when it occurred. And the unsuspecting Tara would think it all perfectly normal.

He noticed a horrid fascination on Jane's face. He took her hand. She looked across at him, worried.

'Are you not worried?' she asked.

'It's different for me,' said Macleod. 'You get caught up in the chase. You can't allow yourself to be worried all the time. Sometimes I think it's like a game. Of course, it's not a game. It all comes back to you in the end, when you realise that someone's dead. To solve it, to stay ahead of it, you can't allow yourself to be thinking that way. You have to get yourself on track. Get yourself teed up, like a game. It's someone's life. How much risk do you take?

'You can paralyse yourself, thinking, don't do that in case it's wrong. Don't do this. When you think it's a game, you make your best bet and you go for it,' said Macleod. 'You've just got to hope that your best bet turns out to be the right one.'

Macleod could hear running feet and turned to see the third officer of the ship, the young Melanie Thatcher, running towards him. He gave her a polite nod of the head as she came up close. Her voice was low, not wishing to be overheard.

'We've got a message from a Detective Inspector Clarissa Urquhart.'

Macleod leaned in closer.

'She says that she believes a Leila Massloe is on board. Leila Massloe used to be Helen Carlisle, and Helen Carlisle was the partner of Johan Reisenberger. She said, 'Reisenberger is dead, but that Helen took his money, and she thinks that they're on board the cruise ship. She spoke to Angela Starry, who's Jenny

Starry's—that's Leila's partner—sister. Angela said that Leila had a new friend, a young man. They're apparently in an open relationship, so they think that's why they came on the cruise.'

Macleod's heart thumped.

'That could be them,' said Jane. 'That could be the last one.'

'Melanie,' said Macleod, 'have we got a room number for them?'

'They're searching through now, seeing who it's booked through. We're not getting anything for a Leila Massloe. As soon as we've got it, though, we'll get it to you. It's just most of the crew are out searching for the person overboard.'

'I understand that,' said Macleod, 'but these people are definitely alive. Well, as far as we know. I need to get to them as well.'

'I'll get back to the Captain. Tell him he has to give as much priority to them as he does to the search.'

Macleod turned and looked out to sea again and then heard a cry from down below. He looked over to the side and realised that a lot of the passengers were looking out of their own balconies. Several of them were pointing now. He saw a lot of the rescue craft converge on a point.

'Have they got something, Seoras? Is that something?'

Macleod looked along the deck and saw a man holding a set of binoculars. He marched across to him, announcing himself loudly.

'I'm Detective Chief Inspector Macleod. I'm involved in this search, sir. May I borrow your binoculars at this time?'

'Yes, here you go, Inspector.'

Macleod wasn't sure if the man was German or Austrian, but he was certainly generous, and Macleod looked through the binoculars out to the sea. As he brought them into focus, he saw the rescue craft stopping alongside something in the water. He then saw what he thought was a body being fished out. He turned and saw a member of the crew up on the upper deck. They'd been scanning. He shouted over to them.

'Detective Chief Inspector Macleod, I'm looking to know where they're going to bring whoever they've found onto the vessel.'

'They'll be able to come aboard down below at the lower decks. I'll take you there if you wish. It's where we use the tenders to go to shore if we haven't got a proper port.'

'Now with despatch, please,' said Macleod. He handed the binoculars back to the German man, giving him a nod. 'Come on, Jane,' said Macleod. 'Let's go and see who this is.'

As he walked away, he turned to another man in white. He was standing beside Mr Ottomeyer.

'Bring Mr Ottomeyer down,' said Macleod. 'We think they've found somebody.' Macleod saw the look of hope in Ottomeyer's eyes and wished it wasn't there. If it was her in the water, Macleod doubted she would be alive.

Macleod quickly followed the junior crew member off the promenade down to the lower decks. Racing through the rows of crew cabins, he was taken through a maze, before suddenly arriving at what looked like a miniature harbour on the side of the vessel. There was a small jetty.

Macleod watched as the rescue craft came in close. The doctor was already there. Macleod hung back, letting the crew go about its business. The doctor jumped on board, one of the rescue craft. Macleod could see him working at someone. Mr Ottomeyer went to race past. Two crew held him back.

'I'm sorry, sir. Let the doctor do what he needs to do. He's what that person needs now.'

'I need to see if it's my wife. I need to see—' Ottomeyer stopped for he saw the doctor stand up. The doctor stepped back onto the small jetty and walked up towards Macleod and Ottomeyer.

'Inspector, I believe you need to come and have a look.'

Macleod walked down the jetty and onto the rescue craft. The doctor turned solemnly to him and said quietly, 'She's dead. The neck's broken. I don't think we could have saved her. It looks like whatever way she hit the water broke her neck. Either that or somebody broke it beforehand.'

'Do we know who it is? Because I have a man over there who thinks it may be his wife. Or rather, I think it may be his wife. I don't know what she looks like, though.'

'Well then,' said the doctor, 'I think the only way you're going to find out is either search her, or ask him to come over.'

Macleod knelt down and saw that the woman had a jacket on. There was nothing on the inside. There was a purse with some bank cards. The name Tara Ottomayer was on them. Macleod gave a resigned sigh.

'I need him to check anyway,' he said. He got up and walked back along the jetty. 'Mr Ottomeyer, I'd like you to follow me. I warn you, prepare yourself for what you will see. We have a dead body on board the rescue craft. I need to know if it's your wife or not. I believe it is, sir, I just need you to confirm it.'

The man looked at Macleod, almost disbelievingly. Then he stumbled forward. A couple of the rescue crew helped him on board the craft. Macleod noticed that the doctor had already covered over the face of the woman. As Ottomeyer drew closer, the doctor asked him if he was ready to look. Ottomeyer nodded. The cloth went back. Ottomeyer stared for a moment, nodded and turned away. By the time the cloth was back over the woman's face, he was in tears.

The Captain appeared, striding down the small jetty and onto the rescue craft. He was about to say something directly to Macleod in front of Mr Ottomeyer, but Macleod held up his hand. 'Captain, I'm afraid we've recovered the body of Tara Ottomeyer. This is Mr Ottomeyer.'

'My condolences,' said the Captain. 'Sincerely, my condolences, but I need to talk to the inspector directly.'

The Captain stepped back off the rescue craft onto the small jetty, indicating Macleod should follow him. Macleod hoped that the man's impersonal nature would be necessary.

'You said you wanted a Leila Massloe. Jenny Starry, Leila Massloe,' said the Captain. 'Well, I've got them. I've got the cabin for them.'

'Where?' asked Macleod. The Captain pulled out a number and a deck. It was about halfway up the ship, and the Captain pulled out a deck plan, showing to Macleod where it would be.

'Take care of this,' said Macleod, 'And Captain, I need an access card for all the doors now.'

'I wasn't going to give you it. I would have to allow access.'

'Captain, I think they're at risk,' said Macleod. He wasn't convinced of it, but with all the activity that had been going on and what was about to happen, maybe the killer would just go for it. After all, everybody else was looking elsewhere. Eyes would be off him at this point.

The Captain almost reluctantly handed over the card that would open all doors. Macleod took off along the jetty, running past Jane.

'Come on,' he said. 'We've got two women possibly in trouble, and anyone who can help, come with me,' said Macleod, running past some of the crew. He didn't wait to see if the Captain would give them permission. Instead, he tore off towards the lift. As he got to it, it was opening with people passing out. Macleod roughly pushed them aside to cries of, 'For goodness' sake, what on earth?'

'Detective Chief inspector Macleod, I need your lift now. Everybody out, I don't care what deck you're going to.'

One man stood still. 'Well, that's rude. I don't care who you are. Frankly, I have been waiting for this lift for the last couple of minutes and I need to get down to—'

Jane stepped into the lift, grabbed the man and physically shoved him out of it. The man's wife went to complain, but she shoved her out too. The door shut as she hit the door-closure button.

Jane looked out at the man, who was trying to step back into the lift. 'You go in between these doors and I'll knock you out,' said Jane. 'I mean it.'

The doors closed over. Macleod pressed the button for the floor he wanted.

'You learned that from Clarissa,' he said as the lift went up. Jane's face broke from a serious stare into a grin. There was nothing to do. The lift would go up at the speed it wanted to. The two of them knew they were about to enter something that could be their worst nightmare.

'Be careful,' Jane said to Seoras. 'We don't know what this is.'

'That's my line,' he said, smiling. 'Don't follow me in; don't take any risks. I'm trained for this. You're not.'

She nodded at him, but Macleod wasn't sure she'd taken it in. 'I mean it,' he said. Promise!'

'I promise,' she said. The door is opened, and they tore off to the cabin they sought.

Chapter 24

Macleod held the deck plan in front of him, turning right and left with Jane behind him.

'It's up here on the left. Up here on the left,' he shouted, as he ran along the corridor. As he got closer to the cabin, he could hear noises inside. 'Stay out here,' he shouted to Jane, taking out the access card that the Captain had given him. He slapped onto the reader, saw the indicator turned green, and pushed open the door.

It jammed for a moment, but Macleod looked down to see a woman lying behind it. Ahead of him, though, in the tight cabin, a man was attempting to throttle another woman. He had his hands around her neck, and Macleod could see she was choking badly. He heaved at the door, stepping in over the prone woman behind it.

'I'm Detective Chief Inspector Macleod. Put her down now. Put your hands behind your head and your knees on the floor.'

The man grabbed the woman, pushing her with all his might, and her head bounced off the rear of the cabin. Macleod tore forward, dipping his shoulder and driving it into the man. The man was younger and rode Macleod's attack, driving his elbow down into Macleod's back. Macleod tumbled into the narrow gap between the two beds.

The man stepped over him, and when Macleod looked around, he was running out of the cabin door. With a quick glance, Macleod looked at the women on the floor. There seemed to be movement from both of them, even if it was slight. He jumped up, leapt out of the cabin door and shouted at Jane, 'Take care of those two!'

'Where are you going?' she asked.

'Did you not see him?'

He tore down the corridor as best he could. Macleod wasn't in the best of shape, but he wasn't that unfit. He saw the man's leg disappear around a corner and ran down after him. He knew Jane was behind him, though.

'I told you to get those women,' he said, stopping momentarily to peer around the corner.

'There's people there,' she said. 'You need help.'

'Enough,' he said. 'You promised.'

Macleod turned the corner, looked along the corridor and saw a door swinging. He ran through the door and found it revealed a set of stairs. He could hear someone running down and followed him. There was a pair of footsteps above him coming down as well, but he didn't have time to think about Jane. He didn't have time to focus on her. Instead, he listened for the footsteps down below.

As he went down, he thought, *maybe six or seven decks.* He saw a door swinging and leapt out through it. It said 'Crew Quarters only', so the man had a key card for that as well. Macleod went through the door and caught a fist in the face. He rocked backwards and barely saw the man disappearing down the corridor. There was blood running from Macleod's nose, but he stood up and ran after him all the same.

'Stop him!' he shouted. 'Stop him!'

He tore past several crew members. Maybe they didn't speak English. Some of them looked as if they were from South America, but Macleod tore his way along regardless, until he went through a metal door that led into a galley. He heard shrieks and yells, and then everywhere went silent.

'I know you're in here,' said Macleod. 'You can't get off the boat. There's nowhere to go.'

'Few have seen me,' said a voice. 'I can disappear. You may have got my cabins, but I can be someone else. With you dead, they won't know what to do. They'll be lost. I've always got another identity I can go to. You remember that.'

Macleod crept down low, walking around the galley. It was huge. There were stainless steel tables in the middle, a larder towards the rear, large freezers, ovens, three or four different sections to walk up and down. Underneath the tables were stored large jars, plastic containers of food. Macleod saw a lot of knives neatly stacked up against the wall on a magnetic fixing. They ran from small up to large, and he saw at the top end the largest was missing. There came a scraping, a drawing of metal on metal.

'Guess what I've got, Inspector? I've got something that stops policemen. Something that keeps you away. I know how to use a knife. Did you know that? I think you did. Durston knew that. Well, he knew that in the end. Did you know Durston put them all up to it? Durston was the one who did it. Or do you know nothing at all?'

'I know you think they cheated you out of money, but you attacked people that had nothing to do with it.'

'Somebody had to pay for their fortune. Johan Reisenberger didn't have the decency to stay alive. Johan wasted money.

Drug addict. I could have been something. Did you know I couldn't get a start? With that money, I would have been up there with them? I would have been up at the top cabins. The top cabins are the best, though. Easiest to get in through the balconies. Did you wonder how I got in?'

'I wondered how you could entertain so many women,' said Macleod, trying to buy time and locate the man.

'You learn to act. You learn to change your appearance. Low-grade acting. Not great. Doesn't pay well. Taught me what I needed to know, though. Taught me how to be anyone. I can age twenty years, but you know that, don't you, Inspector?'

'It's over,' said Macleod. 'We found you.'

'But I've got them, haven't I? When I dispose of you, I'll go back for them. I'll get those women. Leila Massloe. That took a while to spot. She's not Leila Massloe. She's Helen Carlisle, and she wasted that money along with Reisenberger. Johan was an arse. Johan was the worst of them. If she could fall for him, she deserves it.'

The knife screeched along the metal again. Macleod crept forward, down low. He saw a pair of legs. It was two tables away. Suddenly, the man raced forward. Macleod turned, ran around the table, heard a knife clatter behind him. He went to turn to look for it, but it wasn't there, and so backed away again, round another corner, another table's edge.

Part of Macleod thought about reaching for the knives himself, but he wouldn't be quick enough. And besides, when would he ever attack a murderer? He arrested them. They needed justice. They needed to be locked up. He was a policeman after all.

As Macleod crouched, listening for the man, he realised he missed Hope. Hope was good at this sort of thing. Kirsten had been, too. Even Clarissa would have been better. Albeit, she might have picked up the knife and gone at the man, but she was all blood and thunder. Hope was strong, tall. Kirsten, the best fighter he'd ever seen. Ross could even handle himself being a younger man, but Macleod didn't have them.

This was just him. He'd need to be smart. He'd need to be clever, like Clarissa was. Maybe even be dirty. This had suddenly become about survival. Nobody else was coming in to help him, and he didn't blame them. The ship must have been awash with rumour, conjecture about what had been happening. Some of the crew knew people were dead because there were body bags in the temporary mortuary. A makeshift one the doctor would have had set up. Word spread; it always did.

Macleod saw a set of feet walking along the table in front of him. If the man came round that corner, Macleod would be crouched down and facing somebody standing with a knife. As he got closer, rather than turn to run, Macleod whipped his foot round, kicking the man hard in the shin. There was a yelp and Macleod was away, scurrying this way and that way.

He stopped in a gap between two freezers. It wasn't the best place to be. In truth, he'd cornered himself. He tried to peer out down to the right and down to the left. The only line he could see was between the two steel tables in front of him. The man could come from that way. He could come from the left or he could come from the right.

Macleod would have to get back out of this corner, but he didn't want to go prematurely. He didn't want to be out there giving the man a direct sight. Lafferty could throw the knife at him. He wanted to make sure the corridors, so to speak, the gaps between the stainless-steel tables, were clear.

Macleod could see him straight in front of him and there was nobody there. He peered out ever so slowly, looking down to his right. There was no one there. He looked to his left. Again, no one. He went to go, but then the scraping of the knife began.

'Inspector, where are you? You didn't do very well with this, did you? It's a wonder nobody's coming to help you. I thought that's the least they could do after you've helped them. You don't work on the boat, do you? You'll just be on holiday, maybe. It's unfortunate, isn't it? Have you enjoyed your holiday? Was the food good? Did you enjoy getting to see the crime scenes?

'Durston's must have been good. I tried to make him look comfortable. It wasn't easy, having dragged him up to the shower, having cut his throat. I bled him as dry as I could, cleaned it up and dragged him back down. Then away and out the door, out the balcony, up the side of the ship, or rather down to the depths.

'There are ways and means. It took me a long time to figure them out. I've had schematics of this vessel for a long time, worked on it before. I'm not working on it now. Oh, no, I came on separately. I've got one name left, the name you hadn't found. As for keeping five women on the go, I'll be honest, Inspector, it was tiring. I was keen to get rid of Kilmartin early because she was a pain. I was sad to get rid of Carlos, truly a beautiful daughter. Great in the sack too, if you know what I mean. Looking at you, Inspector, maybe that doesn't matter anymore.'

Macleod knew Lafferty was taunting him, trying to bring him back out. He also knew he would have to move, for the man would search and the man would find him. Macleod looked out again. Straight ahead was clear, down to the right was clear. He looked to the left and slowly he crawled out.

Macleod heard a thud on the table beside him. He turned. Half standing up on top of the table, brandishing a large knife, was the man he'd seen in the cabin. The eyes were wild, and Macleod knew the look. But the man had height and Macleod was below him.

Macleod could see it all now. The man would jump. He would fall down on top of Macleod, driving the knife into him, and despite Macleod's hands being out in front of him, he couldn't stop this. This was it. This was Macleod's end.

The knife came forward. Macleod saw the man's knees, the tension. He saw him going to spring.

Then Lafferty was hit, clean in the face. A saucepan had flown towards him. He overbalanced as a second saucepan came towards him. As it hit him, the knife tumbled from his hand. Somebody stepped past Macleod and hit the man full in the face with a frying pan. It was a large one, clearly for cooking for the masses. The man's face exploded in red as he hit the metal table, the blood from his nose running left and right across his face. Macleod desperately scanned the room alongside one of the stainless-steel tables. Now with another pot in her hands stood Jane.

'I told you to stay out. I told you—'

'Seoras,' she said. 'I'm your backup. You said you wanted me with you, and I'm here. He nearly killed you. He nearly—' Jane stepped forward to throw her arms around him, but he stopped her for a moment.

Macleod went over to the man and saw he was stirring. Macleod pushed him over, grabbed his hands.

'Jane,' he said, 'get me some of that. What's that over there?'

'Some twine or something. It's—'

'That will do,' he said. 'Bring it here.'

Macleod tied the man's hands behind him and left him lying on the stainless steel tabletop. He turned and threw his arms around Jane, and she hugged him tightly.

'I will not lose you,' she said. 'Always here for you. I'm always—'

'I know,' he said. 'Thank you, but don't do that again.'

'You have no Rottweiler,' said Jane. 'I know she's your Rottweiler. She's not here. You have no Hope to fight the day. You have no Kirsten. Somebody's got to take care of you.'

Macleod held her tight, looked over her shoulder back towards the man. Miles Lafferty was flinching now.

'We need to get someone,' he said. 'They'll be petrified outside. I need to get him in a brig of some sort.'

He reached up after seeing the blood on her shoulder. *Had it come from his nose?*

'It's over,' he said to her. 'It's over.'

Jane picked up the frying pan again and stood just beside Lafferty. 'Well, go and get someone, Seoras. Get them now.'

Macleod walked backwards towards the nearest door of the kitchen. His eyes focused the whole time, Jane with the frying pan raised high. Lafferty had one eye on it.

Too close, he thought. *Too close.* He opened the door and shouted out for the crew, shouted for people to come in. But calm as he was, Macleod realised that without his team, he really was exposed.

Chapter 25

'Just hold still,' said the doctor, 'cleaning up the last of it.' Macleod had his head tilted back. His nose wasn't quite broken, but it was certainly sore. He'd taken a few punches. He'd had to scramble around that kitchen and his body was sore. It wasn't like when he was twenty running down criminals anymore. He could take it then. These days it got more and more painful, but his face was in a much better state than Lafferty's.

Jane had clocked him properly with the frying pan. The saucepans had hurt, thrown as hard as she could. He was impressed with her. She was feisty as anything and she told him that, at the end of the day, someone was attacking her man. Everything went into it. Every ounce of anger and hate for Lafferty.

That was the thing about Jane. She was candid about things like that. Macleod would have been more disciplined, but then again, he wondered if he would put a frying pan in the man's face if Lafferty was attacking Jane. Maybe he'd have gone at him differently and ended up the victim of the knife. He winced as the doctor seemed to put something which stung on the end of his nose. The doctor stepped back, taking off the latex gloves that he wore.

'I think you'll be fine, Inspector; just let it ease for a bit. I've tended to Lafferty as well. He'll be okay. He'll be smarting for days though from that blow. His nose is broken, pretty smashed up in fairness.'

'Have you made a brig for him?' Macleod asked the Captain.

'Yes, I have. I've assigned people to watch over it. We'll be keeping him in bonds. I've got some of my best people on guard. It won't be that long before we get to port. The authorities there have said they're happy to help secure him until the British government can fly him back. Although that won't take long, will it?'

'I'll get on to my colleague Hope back home, get her to organise. I'll have to do some of it from here, though.'

'You're welcome to stay on with us, of course,' said the Captain. 'Your cruise is booked for the next two weeks.'

'I won't get away with that,' said Macleod. 'They'll want me back. I've got a ton of paperwork to do. The first time I've ever arrested someone on a boat out on the high seas.'

'Well, I thank you for your help,' said the Captain. 'I certainly wouldn't have been able to deal with it without you.'

'I'm just sorry it took so long to get him. We had little to go on,' said Macleod. 'Unfortunately, that's often the case. He worked quickly.'

'Well, he's been talking,' said the first officer, 'telling us the entire story. He's almost delighted with what he's done. Apparently, he was done out of a card game where there was going to be a lot of money. He just wanted to make people pay, he said. It wasn't about getting any of the money back.'

'No,' said Macleod, 'that's what it seems like. Unfortunately, that's one of the hardest to deal with. Lafferty was also very good at disguising himself.'

'He was telling me all about being in a theatre and learning about how people speak. He was changing his voice as he spoke to me,' said the first officer. 'Amazing, it was like he was being a different person each time. Incredible. He said he could do the makeup as well.'

'If you go round the women, the wives and daughter and partners of the victims, I'm sure they'll give you differing descriptions of what he looked like,' said Macleod. 'That's how he did it.'

Macleod looked over at Jane. He was in the corner with a face of concern watching her, and she noticed. 'My wonder woman over there.'

The Captain made his way over to Jane. 'You did incredibly well. Thank you on behalf of the cruise line, myself, and my crew.'

'Don't,' said Jane. 'The team got to the bottom of it. I'm just glad he's come out the other side of it. They look after him, you see. He doesn't think of it, but they're the ones that keep him going, keep him alive. He's getting slower in his old age. Not the brain; it's the body.'

Macleod gave a resigned look, hanging his head, but heard her walking across to him. She tilted his head back up and kissed him on the forehead. 'We got there,' she said. 'We got there.'

'If you don't mind, Captain,' said Macleod, 'I'll come and deal with the formalities later. I need a rest for an hour or two. If that's all right with you, doctor. Good to go, am I?'

'Yes, you are. Don't overexert yourself.' Jane put her hand out to help Macleod to his feet.

'If you want anything,' said the Captain, 'you're at my table.

Just walk in and tell them who you are. Have whatever you want off the menu. Thanks again,' said the Captain.

Macleod nodded and together with Jane walked out of the medical centre until they found the lift. As the doors of the lift closed, Jane realised they were alone. She reached forward, kissing Macleod on the lips. He kissed gently back until realising she wanted more. He felt her arms snake around him. She kissed him deeply and then she stepped back, still holding him but looking into his eyes.

'I didn't realise,' she said. 'I didn't realise how much I loved you until I saw him with that knife. Seoras, I'd kill for you; do you realise that? I'd kill for you.'

'Fortunately, there were no knives around,' he said, 'and you could hit him with a frying pan. We got lucky, or I did anyway. I just see the chase. Could have done with some more people with me, younger men, but they're civilians. That's why I told you to stay back. You're a civilian.'

'No, I'm not,' she said. 'I'm your partner, I'm your Jane. Me, Ross's Angus, Clarissa's Frank, Hope's John. We're all part of you, part of the team. We just pick up the rubbish at home, but nobody was going to take my Seoras from me.' She kissed him again.

'I'll need to talk to the team,' he said, 'and then I'll have a rest.'

'If you say so,' said Jane. She stepped back, and he looked at her, just wondering what she meant. The comment was very half-hearted.

They walked back to their cabin. Once inside, Macleod opened up his laptop in the study. It took him a while, but eventually he placed a call through to Hope. Her picture came up on the screen and after a while she was able to contact Clarissa and Ross, joining him in a video conference.

He heard the shower going, assuming Jane was in there, and didn't feel guilty about being away from her. Instead, he looked at the people in front of him on the screen, including the small image in the right-hand corner of him looking back.

'We did okay,' he said to them. 'We had nothing to start from and I couldn't have got to where I got to without you guys. Thank you; thank you deeply. I'm going to have to have some help, Hope, doing the paperwork. You can phone around from your end. Just make sure we understand what's involved. We get into port in about twelve hours, maybe. The authorities there will take Lafferty into custody. I'll have to sit down and work through exactly how this goes. I've never arrested someone on the high seas before—never had to.'

'How did you stop him?' asked Ross.

'We chased down the cabin of Helen Carlisle. He was in there trying to kill her. I attacked him, but he got out of there. He then stopped me in a kitchen with a large knife. Lafferty was about to kill me when Jane hit him smack in the face. She hit him three times, actually. The last was with a frying pan that broke his nose. There was blood everywhere. I think he was lucky she didn't kill him. She was probably up for it.'

Clarissa clapped wildly and cheered, shouting, 'Go, girl!' Macleod found it a little strange until he saw Hope and Ross clapping too. Then he saw the little picture on the right-hand side. Behind him in a dressing gown was Jane. Her hair was damp, and she was about to lean in over his shoulder.

'He owes me big time,' she said. 'But we got there.'

'Well done,' said Hope. 'At least, I didn't have to look after him for a change.'

'Can I just remind everybody that I'm the Detective Chief Inspector here and you're all my subordinates?'

'I'm not,' said Jane. 'Right, everyone,' she said, looking into the screen. 'I'm afraid Seoras has to have some rest and some relaxation. He thinks he's going to sleep but I haven't really seen him for the last couple of days. Rather, I've hung on to his coattails while he's charged around trying to sort this out. We need some 'us' time, so don't disturb him for the next three or four hours. We'll talk to you after that.'

'Three hours,' said Clarissa. 'You're hopeful.'

Macleod saw Jane stick her tongue out at Clarissa on the screen and then she closed the laptop lid down. Her hand snaked around his neck and ran down the front of his chest.

'The doctor said rest.'

'I don't want rest,' she said. 'I want you. Damn, I hope you're up for it.'

Macleod laughed for a moment. The tension of the entire day running out of his body. 'Yes ma'am,' he said. He leaned back, and she kissed him deeply. 'Us time,' he said. 'Sounds good to me.'

He stood up with Jane taking his hand, leading him back towards their bedroom. As she got to the door, she stopped and turned around.

'The next time I say, let's get away—let's go on a cruise—you tell me no, Seoras Macleod. You send us somewhere which has its own police force and if anything happens, somebody else can deal with it. Okay?'

'Yes ma'am,' said Macleod. Jane turned and pulled him into the bedroom.

Read on to discover the Patrick Smythe series!

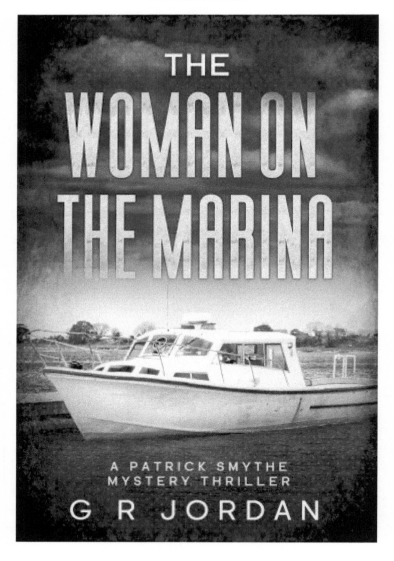

Patrick Smythe is a former Northern Irish policeman who after suffering an amputation after a bomb blast, takes to the sea between the west coast of Scotland and his homeland to ply his trade as a private investigator. Join Paddy as he tries to work to his own ethics while knowing how to bend the rules he once enforced. Working from his beloved motorboat 'Craigantlet', Paddy decides to rescue a drug mule in this short story from the pen of G R Jordan.

Join G R Jordan's monthly newsletter about forthcoming releases and special writings for his tribe of avid readers and then receive your free Patrick Smythe short story.

Go to https://bit.ly/PatrickSmythe for your Patrick Smythe journey to start!

About the Author

GR Jordan is a self-published author who finally decided at forty that in order to have an enjoyable lifestyle, his creative beast within would have to be unleashed. His books mirror that conflict in life where acts of decency contend with self-promotion, goodness stares in horror at evil, and kindness blindsides us when we at our worst. Corrupting our world with his parade of wondrous and horrific characters, he highlights everyday tensions with fresh eyes whilst taking his methodical, intelligent mainstays on a roller-coaster ride of dilemmas, all the while suffering the banter of their provocative sidekicks.

A graduate of Loughborough University where he masqueraded as a chemical engineer but ultimately played American football, Gary had worked at changing the shape of cereal flakes and pulled a pallet truck for a living. Watching vegetables freeze at -40'C was another career highlight and he was also one of the Scottish Highlands "blind" air traffic controllers.

These days he has graduated to answering a telephone to people in trouble before telephoning other people to sort it out.

Having flirted with most places in the UK, he is now based in the Isle of Lewis in Scotland where his free time is spent between raising a young family with his wife, writing, figuring out how to work a loom and caring for a small flock of chickens. Luckily, his writing is influenced by his varied work and life experience as the chickens have not been the poetical inspiration he had hoped for!

You can connect with me on:

🌐 https://grjordan.com

📘 https://facebook.com/carpetlessleprechaun

Subscribe to my newsletter:

✉ https://bit.ly/PatrickSmythe

Also by G R Jordan

G R Jordan writes across multiple genres including crime, dark and action adventure fantasy, feel good fantasy, mystery thriller and horror fantasy. Below is a selection of his work. Whilst all books are available across online stores, signed copies are available at his personal shop.

Scrambled Eggs (Highlands & Islands Detective Book 31)
https://grjordan.com/product/scrambled-eggs
A mysterious attack destroys poultry on an unprecedented scale. Retaliation brings the supply of eggs in Scotland tumbling down. But when the next attack deals a result of human blood, can Macleod and McGrath determine the pecking order to find out who's the fox in the hen house?

When a body is found at the bottom of the latest attack on poultry in Scotland, Macleod finds himself treading through the hen house muck in order to crack open the most scrambled case of his career. Warring factions are absorbed in a melee stirred up by animal rights factions, leaving Macleod with more suspects than feathers. Can the team shift through the hen house remains, and keep the nation's eggs on the table without cracking?

You can't make an omelette without cracking a few eggs!

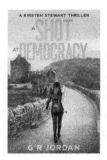

Kirsten Stewart Thrillers
https://grjordan.com/product/a-shot-at-democracy
Join Kirsten Stewart on a shadowy ride through the underbelly of the Highlands of Scotland where among the beauty and splendour of the majestic landscape lies corruption and intrigue to match any city. From murders to extortion, missing children to criminals operating above the law, the Highland former detective must learn a tougher edge to her work as she puts her own life on the line to protect those who cannot defend themselves.

Having left her beloved murder investigation team far behind, Kirsten has to battle personal tragedy and loss while adapting to a whole new way of executing her duties where your mistakes are your own. As Kirsten comes to terms with working with the new team, she often operates as the groups solo field agent, placing herself in danger and trouble to rescue those caught on the dark side of life. With action packed scenes and tense scenarios of murder and greed, the Kirsten Stewart thrillers will have you turning page after page to see your favourite Scottish lass home!

There's life after Macleod, but a whole new world of death!

Jac's Revenge (A Jack Moonshine Thriller #1)
https://grjordan.com/product/jacs-revenge
An unexpected hit makes Debbie a widow. The attention of her man's killer spawns a brutal yet classy alter ego. But how far can you play the game before it takes over your life?

All her life, Debbie Parlor lived in her man's shadow, knowing his work was never truly honest. She turned her head from news stories and rumours. But when he was disposed of for his smile to placate a rival crime lord, Jac Moonshine was born. And when Debbie is paid compensation for her loss like her car was written off, Jac decides that enough is enough.

Get on board with this tongue-in-cheek revenge thriller that will make you question how far you would go to avenge a loved one, and how much you would enjoy it!

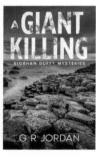

A Giant Killing (Siobhan Duffy Mysteries #1)

https://grjordan.com/product/a-giant-killing

A body lies on the Giant's boot. Discord, as the master of secrets has been found. Can former spy Siobhan Duffy find the killer before they execute her former colleagues?

When retired operative Siobhan Duffy sees the killing of her former master in the paper, her unease sends her down a path of discovery and fear. Aided by her young housekeeper and scruff of a gardener, Siobhan begins a quest to discover the reason for her spy boss' death and unravels a can of worms today's masters would rather keep closed. But in a world of secrets, the difference between revenge and simple, if brutal, housekeeping becomes the hardest truth to know.

The past is a child who never leaves home!